BIRTHRIGHT
:SIERRA'S LEGACY

by Rod Martinez

AcuteByDesign
the little book company that could
A Michael Marion Sharpe Company

BIRTHRIGHT
:SIERRA'S LEGACY

A haunted lake, a girl with a haunted past, and deaths in the family… something in the town of Old Indian Lake, Florida isn't right. Sierra has tragedy in her young life that most people would never know. Orphaned at a young age, she has only vague memories of her family. Sometimes they come in dreams, sometimes in visions. She was left alone, but Sierra was left with a gift—you could call it a legacy—and this legacy completely changed her life around. She's since moved away from the small Florida town with a haunted past, but now she can feel a calling, so she has to go back to Old Indian Lake, where her life changed forever and will do so again.

ISBN 978-1-943515-10-3

Acknowledgments:

The author would like to give a special thanks to author/editors:
Debra Kay Harper and Frank Laumer; editors of THE ENGLISH / SEMINOLE VOCABULARY, a book that proved invaluable in making this story more real to me as I created it. I believe that you, the reader, will also appreciate the hard work they put into the dictionary as you read. Check out their site at http://www.seminolewars.us

This story is dedicated to the Florida American Indian…
the Seminole

PROLOGUE

Residents of the Gulf Coast of Florida know one thing for sure: Hurricane season means you will get rain, and not the happy sprinkling kind. This weekend was worse than most. The tropical storm battered the Tampa Bay area, and yet two enemies stood their ground on the beach on this dark night. Every other Floridian was hunkered down, except for the occasional diehard who thought this the opportune moment to pull out their surfboard.

Sierra was no stranger to massive storms and understood their inherent dangers, yet she stood firm on the beach during the horrible tempest. The cold raindrops pelted down hard all around her, but she wasn't even touched by them. In fact, her long, dry, dark hair flowed against the direction of the brutal wind behind her. Rage was all she felt, and her fury was as big as the storm around her. It was focused on Brooke, her neighbor and enemy in school. Brooke had just received a blow to the face from Sierra—a punch that sent her down to the muddy, wind-beaten terrain. The look in

Sierra's eyes had a greater effect on her than the heavy torrent surrounding them. "Sierra, I'm sorry!" she cried out against the howling wind.

Her voice was hoarse from screaming and being battered by the weather. She slowly stood to her feet, fighting the wind surge that tried to force her back down.

"Brooke, you don't know how to be sorry!" Sierra spat. She wore anger like makeup, and it dripped off her like the rain would have—if the rain were touching her. But Brooke noticed, looking up at her enemy, that though a deep sheet of rain fell from the sky, sideways, it seemed to flow around Sierra without touching her. It was as if her skin repelled the water and forbade it from touching any part of her.

"How are you doing that? You're not even getting wet!"

"Don't change the subject, Brooke; this is the last time I'm going to tell you: Stay out of my business and leave me and my family alone! Do you understand me? You don't know who you're messing with!"

Sierra's dark, angry stare caused a look of fear to come over Brooke's make-up-smeared face. She lowered her head, defeated.

The raven-haired teen turned and walked away, her face wet with angry tears though still dry from the weather surrounding her.

Brooke stood alone on the quickly corroding shoreline, fighting the wind to maintain her footing.

"How is she doing that?"

CONTENTS

CHAPTER ONE

Sixteen years ago

The pain came first in a short spike. She sat on the couch, clutching the huge plush throw pillow and fighting hard to resist the excruciating pangs that hit every few minutes. They'd been waiting for this; it was time.

"Joe! Joe!"

From upstairs, her nervous husband rushed to get to her side, tripping on the staircase on his way down. The heavy thud of his size-10 shoes reverberated within the home, and he caught his footing on the last stair.

"H... Honey? It's not time, is it? Is it?"

He rushed to her and caressed her swollen tummy area, which housed their soon-to-be-born first child.

"Call the doctor, Joe. Hurry, please." Tina screamed.

"The doctor... right... okay, call the doctor, the doctor," he nervously repeated.

He was shaking his hand left and right as if he were holding a phone, then leapt up and hopped for her cell phone, which was sitting on the armrest. As he wiped his already-sweating brow, his forehead instantly became populated with wrinkles. The fear in his face wasn't without cause; a year earlier, his lovely wife of four years had lost their first baby during the delivery, and that left her in the hospital for two weeks.

Tina motioned to get up, struggling hard to get out of the seat. It wasn't easy without a painful grunt and a muscled heave with the help of the soft armrest.

"Oh my God, Joe! I'm bleeding! Oh no. Not again, nooooo!"

Her sobs filled the entire house. He dropped the phone on the floor and quickly decided to hurry her to the car. In one fell swoop he managed to help her up, pulling her, and motion for the front door, and they were already at the door when he remembered the bag. In a panic, he rushed back to the couch, snatched the bag he had packed days before for her, and bent down and grabbed the phone off the carpet without missing a beat.

"We're going to be okay, sweetie," he said, panting as he spoke.

He hopped over the couch to meet her at the door again.

He was determined this time to save his child. Becoming a father was more than a desire since the last ordeal; it had become his obsession, his sole purpose in life, and he wasn't going to let anything get in the way. His wife would have a safe delivery, and the baby would survive if he had anything to do with it.

Half dressed and determined, he sped with his wife out into the street in their sedan. Destination... the hospital.

v v v v v v v

Days had passed. Twenty-five-year-old Joseph Russo sat in his chair, seated in his home office, hair mussed, nervously exhaling a breath of frustration. Married to his high school sweetheart on his twenty-first birthday, he was a young man with a vision, a rarity in pure form. At the age of fifteen, he already knew what he wanted to do with his life and seriously got to work on it, never skipping a beat. He would graduate high school, enroll in computer programming courses, marry his girlfriend, Tina, upon graduation, buy a home, start a home-based computer consulting business, and have his child before reaching the quarter-century mark in his life. Of all these plans, only one would not materialize according to his schedule: fatherhood.

But he wasn't a quitter—no. Joseph David Russo didn't know what it meant to quit. And he wasn't about to learn now. The obsession of having his daughter consumed him like a blaze of uncontrolled fire. He wouldn't give up. And Tina, his wife, shared this determination. They were going to have their first child despite the odds. As determined as the couple was, though, they knew it was a matter of fate—or luck, or whatever they believed in. But truly the child's life would be planned for her before she spoke her first words.

"Joe, can you bring me a glass of cranberry-grapefruit juice, please?" Tina called.

She was in the baby's room and paged him on the intercom they'd installed in advance. After the scare they'd just lived through, where they both thought they'd lost the baby, he had insisted that she follow doctor's orders and rest. The first time they had been ignorant. They did what every parent expecting their first child did: read the blogs, went to Lamaze, connected with other soon-to-be-parents, Pinterest, Twitter—the whole nine; they thought they were in the know. This time they knew better.

He strolled in carefully holding the almost full-to-the-rim glass of her current favorite non-alcoholic drink craving. "Here you are, Buttercup. Cran-Grapefruit on the rocks, hold the olive—just how you like it." He smiled. "Are you feeling better?"

"Yeah... I guess I should just do what the doctor says from now on, huh?"

He placed the glass in her hand.

"Yeah, well she does kinda know what she's talking about, honey. We spent all that time reading blogs and how-tos when all we shoulda been doing was exactly what your OB-GYN told us to do. We don't want to go through an ordeal like we did last year. I want both of you guys pulling through this, okay?"

"Guys, huh?"

"Well, you know what I mean." He caressed her arm.

"Yeah, I know, Joe. So, have you decided on whether or not you're going to attend the seminar at Old Indian Lake?" She took a sip; he'd put too much ice in it, but she wouldn't gripe about it. He'd only offer to bring her a fresh glass of the concoction instead of simply taking a few cubes out.

"I don't know. I mean, it's an important workshop, something that can boost my career big-time. But you're so close and, babe, I just don't want to take a chance, know what I mean?"

"Well, can't I go with you?"

He took a pause and stared at her. The question wasn't something he had expected. She smiled curiously when she asked and put the almost empty glass on the end table.

"Sure, but do you want to? I didn't ask you because I thought you said that all these computer lectures and workshops were boring. Geek conventions?"

"Geek conventions— well, yep, I did call them that. And the workshops are boring, but I can stay in the room or something. I can always text you in case of emergency; I can binge watch one of my shows or just bring something to read. We're still two weeks away from the baby's due date. I can bring my Kindle."

She stared at her husband. Joe Russo stood almost six foot, had green eyes and a short buzz haircut. He moussed the front top of it into an almost-peak.

"So it's settled. You'll come along. It'll be great because then I know you'll get the rest you need. Our cabin is supposed to be state of the art. You'll love it." He paused in a distant smile.

"Babe, our little girl's going to be a beautiful child. She'll have my eyes...."

"My nose, my hair...."

"My sense of humor, my brains...."

"My charm, my cheeks...."

He knelt to his wife, smiling into her.

"You know, Buttercup; the day our daughter is born will be the happiest day of my life."

"Wait,—I thought the day you met me was the happiest day of your life!"

"Okay, well, Sugar Cheeks, it'll be the second-happiest...."

"I thought our wedding was the second most hap—"

"Okay, okay... the third. Geez! You want me to pack for you? I can start with...."

"Uh, no, dear," she interrupted. "I'll do it myself. I remember the last time you packed for me…uh…that was a nightmare, Joe. You have no concept of how women dress."

"Well, I figured the hospital supplied all that stuff! What do I know? I'll go up and pack."

"No, Joseph, the way you dress me, I don't want your computer cronies thinking I'm your grandmother or something. I've got this."

"Okay, Sugar Lips." He shook his head. "Grandmother—the nerve!"

CHAPTER TWO

The drive wasn't a long one. Still, Joseph sat on the driver's side, constantly inquiring about his wife's comfort. To her it seemed like every two minutes, and it got to the point that it was aggravating.

"Are you comfy, sweetie?"

"Joseph David Russo! For Pete's sake, I'm okay. I'm nice and comfortable. I'm fine! I'll let you know when I'm not okay, or uncomfortable, or... anything, okay?"

Geez, my full name. Her quick choppiness quieted her nervously agitated spouse.

"Okay, honey." He sighed.

They turned off the main road, following a yellow painted arrow on a tree.

"Wow, we're here." He smiled.

Approaching the tattered wooden sign, the car tires trampled over noisy gravel as they drove into the quaint cabin resort he had reserved in advance. She read the dilapidated wooden sign overhead as they slowly crept under it.

"Old Indian Lake Cabin Retreat. Wow, Joe this place looks old. What happened to 'state of the art'?"

"Well," he smirked, "… it was state of the art—in the fifties."

As the car slowed down into the dirt-and-pebble driveway, she looked around. There was a huge lake, and a main office, which was built almost exactly like the other wooden cabins sprinkled on the property. There was seemingly no order as to where they were built. They just sat within feet of each other and yards away from the quiet shores of the calm waters. There were enough trees to shade the entire area.

"You know, honey, they say the fish here at Old Indian Lake practically swim up to you, almost daring you to catch them. I sure wish we had time to fish, I'll see what the schedule looks like. I could see you on a boat holding a rod out there, waiting for a bite."

"Joseph, you know I hate fishing…"

"Well then, maybe Nelson and I'll go fishing. Can't take a great lake for granted."

"Nelson? Nelson Vargas? He's coming too? Oh for Pete's

sake, you won't be at the seminar. You and Nelson will probably show up for ten minutes, then disappear into the lake with your rods and reels. Why didn't I see this coming?" She groaned.

"I don't know what you're talking about." He chuckled; then he leaned over, kissed her swollen tummy, and then kissed his wife on the forehead.

"Oh, so the baby gets the first kiss now?"

"Well, you know... she's probably asleep, and I wanted to kiss her good night in there."

"Humph, well, I suppose I'll go swimming later, after you take off for meeting number one. Then I can...."

"Swimming?" he interrupted, "Uh, sweetie, darling, Buttercup, the exertion on your muscles while swimming… uh…I don't think..."

"Joseph, you're becoming my mother! Please!"

"Yeah, but swimming? You're due in two weeks. We'll be here for only three days. Please, just rest here and read. You love reading. You're a librarian, see—I packed your Kindle."

"Oh Joseph..." she shook him off with a wave of the hand.

"Honey, please. Promise me. This is our unborn child we're talking about, you know? After all we've been through, tell me you won't go swimming."

She sighed in despair as he pushed open the door. The cabin keys were on the ring hanging next to the rocking chair, just like he'd been told. She walked in first, slowly looking around the small but comfortable cabin.

"Wow, it's like walking back in time," she told him.

He put the first suitcase on the floor, and then went back for the other stuff. Tina placed her hand on her belly, then walked around inside the one-room cabin. The Keurig was probably the newest thing in the place.

"Quaint," she whispered. "Quaint, but homey in a cute way."

"Ahh, home away from home, huh?" Joe smiled walking in with the rest of the stuff. He dropped her suitcase on the bed, while she slowly placed herself on the small sofa.

"So, you promise, right?" He smiled. "Swimming bad, reading good."

"Okay, den mother. I'll stay right here in our quaint little room, reading articles on 'How to be the good mother-to-be.' Satisfied?" She raised her hand in a mock scout's-honor gesture, rolling her eyes.

"That's the spirit, Honeysuckle." He kissed her. "After all, before we know it, we'll be back home and awaiting the baby's arrival. Okay, so I'd best get off to the first seminar. Remember, text me for anything. Dial the numbers '911' so I know it's baby-related." He handed her the Kindle.

She lip-synched the last sentence with him in a babyish smile; he had recited that line for the past nine months. They giggled together.

"I'll be back."

"I'll be reading." She smiled, folding up on the couch.

He picked up his briefcase and tablet and hurried out the door, making sure to close it shut behind him. She heard the car start and drive off on the gravel roadway. The Kindle was tossed to the bed.

A quick stroll down to the shoreline can't hurt anything.

She was wearing shorts and a maternity shirt and headed for the door. The cabin truly was something built way before she was born, but it had a cute retro look to it. A wall air conditioning unit, an old 27" inch CRT television instead of a flat screen, a kitchen that reminded her of her grandmother's house back when she was growing up, and there was even a VCR under the TV with a shelf nearby of old 1980s movies on tape. The small refrigerator, sink, and two-plate stove reminded her of pictures she'd seen from the fifties. She stopped for a second and looked around the room as if she had forgotten something.

"Hmm, it'll come to me when I get out there. As long as I have the key I'm all right."

She turned the knob and pulled the door open, only to get startled at a figure standing in the doorway there right in front of her.

"Ohh!"

"Hi, Mrs. Russo. I forgot to bring in some extra towels for ya. Your husband had asked for them, I shure didn't means ta scare ya."

"Oh, you're Mr. Kettleman, right? Joe's talked about you several times. I was just going out to the lake."

"Uh, ma'am, are you sure you want to head on out there in your, uh condition?" the elderly gentleman asked in a worried smile, motioning at her belly.

Really?

He was looking at her swollen tummy but quickly shifted his gaze to her face and handed her the towels. She tossed one over her shoulder and dropped the others on the couch near the door inside

"Mr. Kettleman, I'm pregnant, but I can still walk—you know?"

"Oh, sorry—it's just that we men get edgy when we see a woman in your condition, that's all. Kinda confuses us on what to do in the event of, well you know. It gives us the jitters."

"Didn't you have kids, Mr. Kettleman?"

"No can't say as I have. Old Ma and me just never could have children of our own. Plus I was a single child and so was she, so we ain't got any nieces or nephews, either."

He sighed, looking around, then focused on Tina again.

"She passed away, so it's just me now. Don't even know what I'll do with the property should I die. I sure don't want Uncle Sam to have it. This right here is paradise." He smiled. He had stubbled white whiskers that seemed to have not seen a razor in weeks, and a thin, wiry, friendly face. "I didn't mean to offend, Mrs. Russo, about your—uh—you know." He pointed at her belly again.

"I'm not offended," she said, smiling, placing her hand on his, "and the name's Tina."

"Okay, Tina, then I'm Wilbur. If you need anything, just holler. Just don't go out too deep. That's a fresh water lake, and we're in Florida. You know what that means, right?"

"Don't drink the water? Riptide? Loch Ness Monster?"

"Ha. No, ma'am. Gators."

"Gators? Oh, have you seen a gator in these waters?"

"Well actually, no, ma'am, I haven't. Ain't been a gator sighting here ever, as far as I know—and I been here all my life—but'cha can never know. Just sayin'. They're Florida's pet, ya know?" The aged man backed away after a smile and slowly walked off, scratching his head. His worn-out overalls seemed two sizes too big and were frayed at the bottom.

"Well, okay. Thank you, Wilbur."

He stopped, tipped his Tampa Bay Rays baseball cap, and smiled, then turned again and walked away.

"Wilbur." She smiled to herself. "I wonder how Mr. Ed is doing?"

She strolled casually out to the light brown-sanded beach. There wasn't a soul in sight. Such a great day outside, and not a body was on the lake shore. With all of these cabins, people should be taking advantage of this. Northerners would kill for a spot here. We Floridians take our state for granted. She sighed.

She stood at the edge of the lake. The water was calm. She could see the fish springing about, out in the deeper regions. But she wouldn't go out that far; all she wanted was to wade in the shallows. The warm softness of the sand gave way under her feet, and she tipped into the cold water.

"You gonna be okay out there, Mrs. Russo?" called the familiar, elder-sounding voice of Wilbur Kettleman.

"It's Tina! And yes, I will be fine, thank you! Maybe I'll bring you a fish!"

They laughed, and he went back into the office.

Tina waded out a little deeper until the water almost touched her knees.

Wow, this is so relaxing. I think we're going to make this our family vacation spot.

The sounds of nature surrounded her: what sounded like an owl, crickets, and birds singing. The occasional far-off sound of a splash or two caught her attention. The fish seemed to be playing a game of leapfrog just yards away from her.

The soft, warm Florida wind whispered through the tall trees surrounding the compound as the sunlight danced on top of the calm ripples of the smooth lake. Tina's face grew into a slow smile, and soon enough the mother-to-be found herself gently floating atop the peaceful waters of Old Indian Lake.

Wow, this is the life. She sighed. Not a care in the world.

Her sole thought was of her unborn child, wondering how she'd come out once born. She loved her husband's green eyes but also wished that her daughter would inherit her own darker features. She pondered on this, what she'd look like, if she'd favor more Joseph's family than hers. She stroked her swollen stomach area delicately, which brought a soothing smile, a smile that soon slowly faded away as she looked around her lone paradise. She needed a break away like this from life. This was peace. This was tranquility. Floating alone on the calm waters of the lake, she let out a sigh and a smile.

She looked back at the cabin and thought of Wilbur: "Ain't been a gator sighting here ever as far as I know—and I been here all my life—but'cha can never know. Just sayin'."

Hmm, she thought, maybe I should… Then suddenly she was hit with a short, painful burst right where she had placed her hand, on her tummy. She contracted with the pain in a jerk that caused her body to start to sink in the water. "Oh!"

She turned around in the water and glanced for the shore, only to find that it was much farther than she had realized. Struggling to keep her balance, she tried not to panic, but the pain wouldn't allow for common reasoning. She looked down in the water about her; there was blood.

"Oh no… Noooooo! Help! Help me, please! Wilbur!"

The splashing and crying seemed in vain. No one, nothing, not even the vigilant Mr. Kettleman was there to answer her cries. She felt doomed with no possible way out. The pain grew, and she was sure she wouldn't make it to the shore, but she knew that she had to try.

"Tread water, Tina… just tread!" she told herself aloud, in a panic.

It was the most excruciating display of anguish she'd ever experienced. And at a moment where she needed, at more than any time the assistance of another, she felt at her most helpless. Yet, there was something, someone there… she could feel it through her desperation.

She turned, still frantically splashing about in the cool water that seemed to almost savagely drag her in, trying to tread and move toward the shore, which seemed a lifetime away from her. Splashing water blurred her vision for a brief second, and she took in a mouthful of Old Indian Lake as she breathed in.

"Help me, please!" She coughed, choking on the water.

A soft mist started out of nowhere around her. It seemed to emanate from the lake itself. That was enough to scare someone, but she had to keep treading with the hope that Mr. Kettleman was looking out his window. Then she thought she saw a hand outstretched to her. It was a dark, masculine hand, reaching out in this, her most dire moment of need. She splashed in horror as the water-drenched hair in her eyes denied her a clear view for the moment, but she reached out.

The mist grew dense and almost looked like fog. It rolled in mysteriously and covered her and her guest on the lake.

"Please…." She reached out.

The hand pulled her up and onto a floating vessel of some sort. The cold, wet hair in her eyes was still blocking her view, but there, in the middle of the vast body of water known as Old Indian Lake, she was brought up to safety—and just in time. She tried to keep calm, but the agony was too much, and it was getting much worse really quickly. She began to hyperventilate. She peeked through painful eyes at her rescuer: an aged Native American, who returned a solemn glare back at her.

"Please, please... take me back to shore! I'm having a baby!"

He finally pulled her fully into the small canoe and placed her to rest against the dry cloth bedding. She wasn't even sure he understood what was going on, much less how she'd get to a hospital in time.

"Do you understand? Boat? To land? Over there? Please hurry!"

Her hands were thrashing in the air savagely, but he remained calm. He reached down and caressed her womb through her belly with an experienced hand. Tina was taken aback by his action, but for some reason, whatever he was doing was working. The pain seemed to slowly abate. She could feel that the baby was coming, and there seemed no way to get to shore, much less to the hospital, or get in touch with Joseph in time.

"My phone! That's what I forgot!" she cried, though surely, soaked from the lake, it wouldn't have worked anyhow. "Mr. Kettleman!"

There was no alternative; she knew she was going to have this baby right there in the middle of Old Indian Lake, in a canoe of all things!

The old Indian, sure and confident of what he was doing, knelt on the boat, silent through her screams of pain, and kept his serious posture, all the while preparing her for the delivery. He began chanting as he helped her prepare. It was now or never, and they both knew it. But he was calm, and his calmness helped her relax as much as she could through this ordeal.

The pain was unbearable, but she remembered everything she'd learned in Lamaze. He motioned for her to push, and she did, with all her might. All the while, he'd placed his hand at strategic points of her legs and vagina, continuing his chanting. It was obvious he knew what he was doing, and this reassured her somewhat. Still… in a canoe!

Then she felt a heaviness overcome her, a cloud of peace that gradually rendered her unconscious. It felt like the weight of a heavy quilt had covered her entire body. She went from warm air and cold water to the sensation of soft, cool, calming and stillness.

The air around the boat chilled quickly. Where, just minutes before, the warm Florida air had blown over her skin, now it had changed temperature radically. It actually felt good to her. The stillness of the water and soft, cooling breeze were one with her, giving the aged Native American the ability to help her all the more. She felt no more pain and wasn't sure if she was awake or dreaming. And the cloudy fog got thicker by the minute.

Suddenly the cry of a baby filled the still air, a cry that echoed within the enclosed panorama of ice-blue water and serene shrubbery surrounding it. The cry awoke Tina from the spell she was under, and she jerked upward in shock on the small canoe. The Indian held the newborn in his hands, raising it above his head, speaking utterances only he could understand. As he spoke, all of nature around him silenced. Only his deep baritone could be heard, along with the steady cry of the child. Then far in the distance, by the howling of a wolf, or at least to Tina it sounded like a wolf or some wild animal far in the distance, accompanied the baby's cry.

"My baby... let me see my baby."

She glanced back up at the man who had helped her give birth. He shined a proud smile at her and lowered the baby into her arms. It was an emotional moment for everyone on that small vessel. The baby cried, Tina cried, and a single joyful tear shone in each of the Seminole's eyes.

"Sierra, oh Sierra... you're so beautiful. " Tina smiled, even as she was sobbing.

The Indian reached over into the water with his hand and brought up a scoopful. He slowly leaned over to the mother and child, placed one hand on the baby's head, and poured the handful of water over the child.

"Is-tah-chee owewah," he uttered softly.

Tina felt another powerful peace overcome her, and within seconds, she and the baby were asleep.

CHAPTER THREE

"Is-tah-chee-owewah." The word, or phrase—she wasn't sure which it was or what it meant—stayed locked in her brain. It bounced around in her head.

She could sense that she was being watched, yet in the stillness of peace she was in, she found it hard to open her eyes. Sound slowly faded in, at first in gibberish mumblings; then it came into recognizable form as the voice of her husband.

"Are you sure she's going to be okay?! God, I knew I shouldn't have left her alone.. I knew it. We should have stayed home. We should have! I'll never forgive myself…"

"Mr. Russo, she's perfectly fine—just in a daze, that's all."

"Babycakes? Honey, can you hear me? Please, wake up, baby. Please wake up."

Her hand twitched. It was a nervous tingle she felt, almost like an electric shock had started from her spine and shot out to every limb. She opened her eyes, slowly, painfully trying to fix focus on the first thing in her sight. The blur gave way to vision.

"J… Joe?"

"Honey, are you okay? I—I don't know what I'd do if—"

"Baby… my baby… where's the baby?"

"Your baby is fine, Mrs. Russo. She's in another room." The doctor smiled, approaching the other side of the bed, "…you know, you've become quite the celebrity up here. A self-induced labor, expertly administered by yourself, in the middle of a lake. This has got to be a record of some sort."

"Sierra—Joe, is she…?"

"She's fine, sweetness. She's beautiful… just like you. She's a hit with the nurses."

"Joe, how did I… the Indian…."

"Mrs. Russo, you really need to rest. Save your strength. You'll be able to go home in the morning. But right now, relax, don't talk… just relax." The nurse smiled.

"I'll be right back, Buttersnaps," her visibly anxious husband reassured. "I'm just going to go back and check on Sierra. I'm staying here with you tonight. Everything is going to be fine."

She motioned to talk again, but he covered her lips with his in a gentle kiss.

20

"Shhhh. I'll be right back."

He turned and walked out, following the doctor.

The serenity of the hospital room brought a peace to her, a peace she had felt once before, on the lake. Her eyes were closed, but she felt another presence in the room, and the sudden aroma of incense filled every inch of her closed quarters. Again the word, or phrase, repeated in a whisper in her head: "Is-tah-chee owewah."

"Joe? Joe?" she called.

She heard a brief rattle near the door, and she tried but couldn't open her eyes. An essence passed over her, a brief heaviness pressed against her, but she felt no form of any kind, just a heavy pressure that held her against the bed for a split second. Then it left.

"Joe! Joe!" she was pushing the nurse call.

The door rushed open without hesitation.

"I'm here. Are you in pain?" He walked in with a nurse.

"Joe... the Indian, the old Indian—what happened to him? Did he bring me here?"

"Old Indian? Why no, Sweetcakes, Wilbur Kettleman brought you here. Don't you remember? He found you and the baby in a canoe on the shore. Don't you remember anything from ...?"

"Joseph, there was an Indian!" she cried between gasps, "An old Indian man who pulled me out of the water. He was there, he did the delivery. I would have drowned if it weren't for him! We would have lost Sierra!"

"Sweetheart, you've just come through a traumatic experience. God knows I wish I would have been there. I'll never forgive myself, but..."

"Joe, don't humor me! I know what I experienced, for Pete's sake. There was a Native American man, and he came in a mist, and he...!"

"Okay, okay, honey, I believe you." He smiled reassuringly. "He delivered our daughter in the middle of Old Indian Lake, in the mist, right?"

"Oh, Joseph, just leave! Please, just go!"

"But Dumpling..."

"Please Joe!"

She turned away with a deep, angry sigh. He stood, lovingly swept a caring hand over her forehead, and slowly headed for the door. It shut behind him on its own. Within minutes, she was fast asleep again. The nurse covered her, then shut off the light, passing a paper calendar on the wall with a scene of the lake and an old Seminole in a canoe.

CHAPTER FOUR

"Push, Tina, push!"

"Oh! Aaargh!"

"The baby, here she comes, okay, rest... breathe," the doctor said.

"Oh Joe... it hurts... Joe!"

"Just a little more, hon, just a little more—right, Doc?"

"Tina, we're almost there. Don't give up on us now." The doctor breathed as the nurse wiped his brow.

"Okay," she uttered under a painful sigh.

"Push!"

"Ohhhhh!"

Along with her painful shrieks there coincided another cry, the cry she had longed to hear throughout this ordeal. The proud father stood firm, clasping his weary wife's trembling hand, and wiped her sweat-sheened face.

"Joseph, Tina...it's a girl."

Within minutes, Joseph Russo was strutting out into the waiting area, big smile and handful of lollipops, almost tripping over a bench on the way.

His mother, friends, and his co-worker and partner Nelson waited anxiously.

"Congrats, bro." Nelson smiled. They bumped fists.

Joe, still in his perspiration-drenched garb from the delivery, hopped over first to the quiet little girl in the corner, busily coloring a picture of a surfer on a tidal wave in her hospital-issue coloring book. Of all the pictures in the twenty-four-page book, it was the one that stood out to her. The little artist was only three years old. Her father picked her up in his arms, and the solemn child's face glowed with excitement as soon as she saw him.

"Sierra, you have a baby sister!"

The entire room burst into cheers, but of the many pats on the back and handshakes and hugs he received, none was as dear to him as the kiss he got from his three-year-old daughter.

"A baby sister?! What'll we call her, Daddy!?"

"It's up to Mommy, Sierra. After all, I named you."

* * *

The new family was home in two days. Sierra was very inquisitive about every little sound and movement her baby sister made. Joe was so responsive to his wife's needs it became almost sickening to her, but she did enjoy the pampering.

"Okay, so I have the menu for today. Chinese. I ordered online. It should be here within half an hour. Babe, I think maybe you should get ready for your soothing bubble bath. I'm fixing the tub for you right now. Which scent do you prefer?" He pulled out three different bottles.

"Uh, surprise me, Joe."

"Mommy, can I pick? I like the purple one." Sierra smiled.

"Purple it is, then." Joe chuckled on his way out. "Purple suds, purple soap in purple water for my purple pop-princess."

"Daddy is so silly." The little girl chuckled.

"Yeah, get used to it, Sierra."

* * *

A month passed. The young family was getting used to the new schedule of life. Those thirty days had come around far more quickly than any of them would have liked. Joe and Sierra were driving into the parking lot of MooMoo's Daycare. This was to be Sierra's first day in daycare. It was a big deal to her and her father.

"You're a big girl now, Sierra. While Mommy goes back to work and I open my new office, you have to be a good girl and follow the rules here at your new school. Okay?"

"I know, Daddy. But why can't I stay at Gramma's with Breanna?"

"Because this is the start of your future. You're going to school now. You're my big girl. And you're going to do great because you're really smart for your age. So have a good day in school, okay? I have to go meet Uncle Nelson. We're opening our new business, and that means I'll be able to drop you off and pick you up every day. Yep, we'll be riding buddies. Ain't that cool?"

They walked into the office, Sierra held her Tiara Wars lunch box close.

"Don't worry, Dumplin'. You're going to do great. You come from a long line of geniuses, you know?"

"Geniuses? I hear Mommy call you that all the time when you're not around." She smiled.

"Hmm, what else does she call me when I'm not home?"

Little Sierra thought about it, then smiled and said, "Okay, I'm ready to go in now."

He opened the door, and they walked in.

CHAPTER FIVE

Twelve Years Later

She felt the water climbing, it was already up to her nose, and she was treading as best as she could, but it didn't matter. The under-current was pulling her down. She took in another quick gasp and went under. She opened her eyes in the murky water and saw two red eyes staring back at her, with a dark wrinkled hand reaching out to her. Try as she might, she couldn't swim away fast enough, and the current was pulling her into the depths.

Nervous bubbles exited her mouth, and she fought hard

to fight the current. Then the dark hand grabbed her ankle, and she bent down to free herself, only to find the face of a dead man staring back at her.

"Aughhh!"

Her scream woke her out of her nightmare. The teenager sat up on the bed in a cold sweat, and her door quickly burst open. He ran to her side.

"Sierra! Are you okay?"

She was sitting up on the bed. Tears started, and she was frantically panting. He sat on the bed and held her in a hug.

Sierra was fifteen years old now, a beautiful young woman, but she had an issue, and it haunted her daily. She reached over and flicked on the lamp on the nightstand next to her bed, then held him in a strong hug. "Uncle Nelson, I keep having these dreams…."

"I know, sweetheart."

He rose from the bed side and pulled the shades on her window. She could see the sunlight sprinkling in. She stepped up from the bed and walked over to the window, looking out. They lived in a condo high-rise in St. Petersburg Beach, Florida. Their "back yard" was the beach, a haven to tourists from all over.

She stood and pressed her hand against the window, staring at the water. "Uncle Nelson?" She turned and looked up at him, and he already knew what was coming next: the dreaded questions from her haunted past.

"Yes, honey?"

"Uh, when Mommy and Daddy and Breanna died, did they…uh, did Daddy…?"

"Sierra, honey, please stop doing this to yourself."

She turned to him, eyes swollen with tears, then looked out of her window over at the beach again. The shoreline was a sight most people loved, but she despised. She had her reasons.

"I… I can't, Uncle Nelson."

"Do you want to go see the doctor again? I can call him, set up an appointment."

"No, I don't think that helped at all. He asks so many questions that have nothing to do with—well, helping me."

"Okay. Well, I have to go see a guy about some networking job. You want to come with me or stay? We can stop for breakfast over at The Egg and I. It's your favorite." Changing the subject was something he was always prepared for.

"I'll stay. Thanks, though."

He held her in a hug, wiped away her tears, and kissed her on the forehead. "You're going to be okay. It was just a dream. Keep telling yourself that. Okay, Sierra? It was just a dream. You know, the other night I had this weird dream. I was at the zoo at Lowry Park in Tampa, and a monkey snatched my phone and started taking pictures of me!"

"What? What happened then?"

"Well I conned him into giving me back my phone, and when I looked at the gallery, all the pictures were of another monkey."

She started to giggle, more so from the funny face he made than the actual story. "What are you trying to say— you're a monkey in real life?" She laughed.

"I'm still trying to remember if there was another monkey in the cage with him when he snapped those pics."

"You're just being silly. You didn't really have that dream, did you?"

"Of course I did. Who lies about dreams? Anyway, when I get back, maybe we can talk about a vacation or something. I know of a family that owns a cabin in the mountains of North Carolina. You'll love that—you've never seen mountains before."

"Okay, Uncle Nelson." She smiled softly.

He grabbed his phone and closed the door behind him, and she turned and stared out the window again. Sierra had a beautiful face. She looked a lot like her mother. Tina was Hispanic, so Sierra had her mom's olive-toned skin, long, dark hair, and huge, watery dark eyes. Her face looked older than what would be expected of a fifteen-year-old; she displayed an essence of tenderness, yet maturity at the same time. Her smile was a beautiful one, but she was always so sad. She glared out at the water from her window; a tear slowly welled up in her eye. As she stared out, her vision went hazy because a flashback had started in her head. It was a vision she could not stop if she tried, and she did try, countless times. Now it seemed she was about to relive the tragedy in her mind all over again…

$$* \; * \; *$$

At age ten, while she was on a family vacation at Old Indian Lake, the small Florida town that would eternally stay locked in her mind, her life had changed forever. Ever since she was born there, her parents had decided that it would become the family vacation spot, and Wilbur Kettleman became a close and dear family friend. They returned every year, but when she was ten, something happened. Everything changed. Her life changed. Reaching age ten is supposed to be a milestone in every kid's life, but for Sierra, age ten was when she became an orphan.

She closed her eyes as tears crept from them and down her cheeks. In her mind she saw it happen as if it were yesterday. The family was in a canoe on the lake. There were other families out there, too. Little Sierra and her baby sister were rowing, while their dad played guitar in the boat and their mom sang. This was as picturesque a scene as one could imagine: Norman Rockwell material.

Then Breanna saw a fish in the lake. It swam right up to the boat, showing no fear of humans. It looked like a huge goldfish. "Look, Mom, a fishy!" she squealed. The seven-year-old got up and tried to touch it.

"Breanna, get back in the boat!" her mom scolded.

"But it's a big goldfish, Mommy. See?"

She leaned over, tried to reach, but the fish backed away. She leaned farther, lost her balance, and fell into the water. Her mother screamed. Her father threw the guitar aside; it landed in the water on the other side of the boat. He dove in after her, and in seconds both of them sank.

Tina turned to Sierra. "Honey, stay in the boat!"

She dove in. Sierra saw bubbles… and nothing else. "Mommy!? Daddy!? Breanna?"

She looked all around her, waiting for one of them to emerge from the lake, but instead a group of fish swam up to the boat and was staring at her. She looked around for help, and to her surprise, suddenly all the other families that had been out there were gone; the only thing on the water was herself in the canoe and her father's guitar, which slowly floated off. She knew there had been other people out there with her. Where had they gone?

"Mom? Dad? Breanna? Hello?"

No one replied. She was alone out in the middle of Old Indian Lake.

"Nooooo!" she screamed.

Wilbur Kettleman heard the scream, and he ran out from the cabin office to the shore. He witnessed the ten-year-old girl jump into the water from the boat, then there were ripples, and the ripples got bigger and bigger to the point that waves started to form. He heard some kind of scream from underneath the water, and then he saw Sierra float back up to the top, still screaming—and she was standing straight up, as if something or someone was lifting her—and the water split apart around her.

A huge wave started and was headed to the shore right where Wilbur stood. It grew larger, the faster it came toward him. It almost seemed possessed with some sort of life, and he ran back, frightened, to the door. When it finally splashed against the shore in a big, horrible crash, the sound was reminiscent of a horrendous thunderclap, so common in Florida during thunderstorms. Then it slithered back humbly into the lake. Joe Russo's waterlogged guitar crashed against the sand and burst into pieces, but as Wilbur raised his hand over his eyes to look out into the lake, ten-year-old Sierra was gone.

* * *

She stood there, staring out the window in her Uncle Nelson's apartment, trying to fight off the flashback from her mind. She'd been haunted by it for years. Her only surviving relative at the time was her grandmother, and Gramma suffered a heart attack the minute she found out about the family tragedy. That left little Sierra in the sole custody of Nelson Vargas, her dad's best friend and business partner, and her godfather. A confirmed bachelor, Nelson wasn't sure how he would handle his new-found duties, but he was going to give it his best shot, for sure.

BRZZZT!

The doorbell made her jump; she wiped her eyes, gradually making her way to the door and squinted through the small peep-hole. A familiar face stared back. She pulled the door open, and the handsome young African American teen stood there, brandishing a huge smile.

"Hey, Sierra, what's up?"

"Not much, Joey. Uh…I was just waking up as a matter of fact."

The sixteen-year-old was checking her out. It was something she was used to having happen with most guys, anyway, but she'd known Joey for the five years she'd lived here. He was the son of the principal of her school. Having known her for all these years, he might have been expected to have gotten over her looks by now, but he never had. The star high school quarterback reminisced over the first time he had met her, at school orientation.

$* * *$

"Okay, class," the burly teacher with a thick New England accent barked. "You've all been through this rodeo before. Your agenda books need your information on the first page, and please don't make me look over your shoulders; let's start this year off right."

"He says the same thing every year," Joey whispered to Sierra. She was sitting right next to him and very nervous about her first day in a new school. Nelson had to make a bathroom run, so she sat there looking lost to everything around her in the auditorium. Starting in a new school was the last thing she wanted to have to live through or deal with, having just buried her family.

The blonde sitting on her other side brushed against her.

"Oops, pardon me, are you new? I'm Brooke—you know, like Brooke Shields? I was named after her. After all, back in her day she was a high-paid model, then actress. Pretty much what's going to happen to me once I graduate high school in a couple of years. Did you tell me your name?"

"No, I didn't." Sierra shrugged.

"Oh well, I'll catch you sometime. Make sure you join the Selfie Club. I'm president. Everyone wants to be in my club." She turned to two girls who were just walking in.

"Oh, Ashley, Brittney…here I am." She walked down to them as the teacher once again rapped his fist on the podium.

"She's really into herself, isn't she?" Sierra said, motioning to Joey. He was staring into her, but she didn't even notice. She had her hand in her backpack, searching for a pencil.

"Huh? Yeah, Brooke thinks she's going to be a movie star. We just humor her."

"And remember lunchtime is a time to eat, not socialize," the teacher continued. "You have thirty minutes to get your food, eat it, and put your trays away, so do yourselves a favor and put your phones away when the lunch bell rings and scarf your food down. You'll need it!"

"He sure seems like he's a strict teacher," she said to Joey. She didn't even acknowledge him with her eyes.

"Nah, Mr. Brick is okay. He just don't like kids. He even opened up and said that last year to a class."

"Well, he's in the wrong profession, wouldn't you say?" She smiled.

She finally turned to him. He had started to say something but got caught in her gaze. Try as he might, he was lost in her dark, brooding eyes. He stared at her long, silky black hair and that smile that seemed right off the cover of Seventeen magazine. He just froze, and the only thing that could exit his mouth was…

"Uh…"

"Hi. I'm Sierra." She smiled.

"Uh…"

"Uh? Well Uh's an interesting first name."

"Huh? Uh, no, Joey. My name's Joey. Uh…"

"Joey Uh. Okay, interesting last name."

He shook his head in frustration, not believing that he'd zoned out at this moment. The timing was perfect because Nelson shuffled in and sat beside her in haste.

"Sierra, honey, did I miss anything?"

"No, Uncle Nelson, nothing at all. Oh, this is Joey Uh."

"Uh what?"

"Nothing, just Uh."

Nelson stared at the young teen and arched one eyebrow. Joey slapped his forehead after she turned around.

* * *

The young athlete now standing at the door shook his head with a smile, staring at her.

"Hello, earth to Joey?"

"Oh, yeah—uh…we're all going to Brooke's condo. Her parents are off in DC, big party. Kelsey's bringing her DJ equipment. It's gonna be off the chain. Wanna come?"

She stared at him for a second, smiled. Brooke always threw wild parties. Her parents were rich. The beach condo was just one of the homes they owned.

"I'll think about it. Uncle Nelson just left, and I—" BREEP! The phone cut her off in mid-sentence. She waved him off; he blew her a kiss and walked away after the door slowly closed shut.

"Hello?"

"Hello, uh—is this Sierra?"

"Yes?"

"Uh, this is, um, hey, well, is uh, is Nelson there?"

"No, he went to see about a job thing. He shouldn't be long. May I take a message?"

The voice hesitated. The mature male voice on the other line seemed nervous.

"Uh…"

She fidgeted on the phone and walked back over to the

window.

"Uh, well… this is Wilbur. Uh, you know, Wilbur Kettleman—remember me? How are you doing, Sierra?"

"Mr. Kettleman? From Old Indian Lake?"

"Uh, yeah. I really need to talk to Nelson. It's all kindsa God-awful important. Do you have his cell phone number? I seem to have lost it. I got a new phone, and all my addresses and stuff are gone. These dad-gum cell phones…. I had your phone number scribbled in my desk. Wasn't even sure you'd still have this number. Thank God you answered. Uh, can I get Nelson's number?"

"Sure. You have a pencil?"

She could sense something was really troubling him, and she was dying to ask what it was but didn't know how to broach the subject. She hadn't seen him since she was ten, when… it happened.

"Okay, I'm ready."

"Ok, area code 727…."

She heard keys jingling outside the door; then the door burst open. Nelson hopped in, dropped the things in his hands on the couch and ran straight for the bathroom.

"Oh, Mr. Kettleman, he just walked in. Uh, he'll be with you in a moment."

She chased him to the bathroom and handed him the phone. He slammed the door as soon as he stepped in.

"Hello? Oh Wilbur, man, how the heck are you?" Nelson was struggling with his belt with one hand while he held the phone up to his ear. "What? What do you mean you saw… oh… oh man… uh, when?"

He yanked at his pants and shoved them to the floor.

Outside, his goddaughter could hear the buckle fall, then his weight slam down on the toilet seat and the sounds of gasses escaping from his body.

"Oh my…" She grimaced, waving her hand past her nose. Sierra stood by the door, put her ear against it, and held her nose.

"What do you mean, you saw them? That's impossible, Wilbur. You can't have seen them. They're dead! Come on, man—this isn't a good time to be joking about this kinda thing!"

Sierra gulped at the door. Her eyes widened in hungry curiosity. She had to know what they were talking about.

"Look, Wilbur, I'm sorry. I didn't mean to insinuate that you were lying, but…I know, I know. Look if you've been drinking again… no? You quit drinking? Wow, congrats, man. I know it musta been hard to do. So, well, what did the police say? Geez, Wilbur, okay, okay… I'll head straight out. I have to go there anyway next week for a job thing. Are those developers still in town? They wanted a quote but wanted me to be there in person. Okay, cool, but I don't know how I'm going to explain this to her. No, I don't want her to come. Are you kidding? I can't bring Sierra back to Old Indian Lake. Do you have any idea what that would do to her? I'll have to figure it out. Bye." He got up.

She heard the flush, and she walked away from the door and hurried to her room. Minutes later Nelson walked out of the bathroom and was spraying it with Febreze. He suffered from bad indigestion. The doctor said it was I.B.S., and at any given moment he could be stirred to have to run to the bathroom. It was something he had dealt with for the past five years, and Sierra just had to get used to it. If they went out somewhere, she knew to expect to look for the closest bathroom for him. It was a responsibility she'd taken on herself since she started living with him. He was in his mid forties and was about the same age Sierra's dad would have been had he been alive. They'd been best friends and eventual partners at work.

Joseph-Nelson Network Storage Solutions became a known name in the Tampa Bay area for any computer network backup type job need that small businesses and banks craved. They had a keen sense concerning what their clients needed and delivered in a very timely manner. Nelson's mind seemed almost to work like a computer at times, and that was what made him and Joe—Sierra's dad— best friends. He had salt-and-pepper hair that contrasted with his naturally tan skin, a stocky, muscular build, and a slight Hispanic accent. He loved chocolate milk. Chocolate milk was the only thing Sierra and Nelson had in common. He was an extroverted businessman, she a shy, introverted teen still haunted by her past.

She lay on her bed thinking about what she had heard. What could Wilbur have seen that shook her uncle up so badly that he would leave now to visit him at her place of birth? Being in the business he was in, he constantly got requests from contractors and architects for new projects in and around Tampa Bay, but his name had also made it out to other towns, and a developer in Old Indian Lake had requested his expertise. He was slated to meet these developers at a later date, but now, because of Wilbur's call, it seemed he'd be meeting with them sooner. Sierra was determined to find out what was happening. She wasn't going to let this go.

Nelson hurried to his bedroom to throw together a quick overnight bag for his drive. With his condition, he knew he could never just hop in a car and go. He had to prepare. While standing near the bed throwing several shirts into his bag, he looked over at the dresser. The picture of Sierra's eighth grade dance stared back at him.

He sighed, dropping the socks on the bed.

"How am I going to leave and not let her know where I'm going? She's been asking to go back to Old Indian Lake for years. But I can't bring her back there. Just the idea of her standing on the edge of that lake—it would kill her. I have to think of something quick."

Finally packed, he opened the bedroom door.

"Sierra?"

The condo's living room seemed unnaturally quiet. Usually at least the TV was on. It wasn't until he approached the kitchen that he noticed the pink Post-It note on the counter.

"Sierra?"

He took the note, still looking around, listening for some sign of her. He reached for his glasses. Pocket left, pocket right, front shirt pocket.

"Geez!"

He wiped his brow in frustration and found them on his head.

"Uncle Nelson," it read, "I went out to the beach with some friends, I'll be back tonight. Don't worry about dinner. I'll eat out."

He pulled a Sharpie out of the pencil cup and turned the paper over, then scribbled, "Sierra, something's come up, with work. I'll be back home tomorrow. Don't forget to take out the garbage, Love you… Unk."

He slammed the paper back on the counter and rushed to his room to change.

"This is perfect. If she knew where I was going, it'd be Hell. She'd beg me to let her come, and I'd have to fight her; then she'd cry, and I'd give in and be miserable because of the pain she'd go through. I think I'd better hurry and get the heck outta Dodge!"

In no time he was tossing his overnight bag into the back seat of his black Hyundai, and then hopped in the car and took off. He didn't know exactly what to expect, but he was going to have to do this. Whether he liked it or not, he had to get to the bottom of Wilbur's frantic mystery. His next destination: the small town of Old Indian Lake.

CHAPTER SIX

Old Indian Lake was a very small community. It was about forty miles north of St. Petersburg, straight up the Gulf Coast. Most small Florida towns looked the same. They were formed either during the Spanish conquistadors' times, early 1800s, or turn of the 20th century.

Nelson loved the old town, but he couldn't ever visit again because of Sierra. Speeding up the highway, he revisited in his mind meeting Joseph David Russo, who became his best friend, at a seminar on a new innovation everyone was calling simply "the cloud." The two young, ambitious men formed an instant bond. They had the same goals, the same ideas, and the same dream. And as a team they made it happen. Joseph-Nelson Network Storage Solutions, or simply "Joseph Nelson," as they liked to call their small firm, was the leader in online data backup solutions for most businesses in the Tampa Bay Area. Sure, they had some other clients from across the state, including a stint when they worked as an offline branch of NASA's security files, but the bulk of their business was in the Bay area. They specialized in backing up network data, storage, files, whatever the client wanted onto their securely encrypted servers. Their clients could always count on Joseph Nelson to be there when they needed. Come hurricane season, when the fierce storms hit Florida, their servers would go into overtime, but no client of theirs had ever lost any data or information. Their secure cloud service was hard to beat.

The idea for this all came about at that fateful seminar at Old Indian Lake, back when Sierra's mother was carrying her. Old Indian Lake became the family vacation spot and the prime location that Joe and Nelson would go to to brainstorm new ideas. Wilbur Kettleman had morphed from old stranger to close friend to both of them and always made room for the partners. The small community really only served as a convention center for businesses looking for the Florida climate but wanting to get away from the hustle and bustle of Tampa, Orlando, Miami, and other busy towns. To visitors, it was true old Florida: peace, palm trees, flamingos, a quiet lake, and a convention center in the middle of the town. It seemed everyone in the town either worked for the center or served in other businesses that supported it. It was a town put together in the fifties, though it seemed way older than that.

The drive wasn't as long as he'd remembered it, but Nelson had a lot going on his mind. As the blurred picturesque scenery sped by his window, he drove in sincere concentration. He worried constantly over Sierra. He struggled at times, juggling both jobs of being a parent and running a business. He had no social life because of this. And now, to add to the frustration, this trip happened all because of a crazed phone call. Not that he didn't have to come back here anyway; the business venture he had been asked to consult on there in Old Indian Lake could be lucrative enough to set him up for early retirement, and he liked that idea. Although the meeting was set for next week, he worked on the idea that maybe he could push it to today and kill two birds with one stone. A developer had plans to put the town of Old Indian Lake on the map, and Nelson was always about improvement, especially if it concerned his business. Wilbur Kettleman had put in a good word for Joseph Nelson, and they were quick to act on it. Plus it would come as a Godsend two fold for him: he could spend more time with his beloved "niece" Sierra and concentrate on helping her with her demons.

The black Hyundai parked up at the cottage, and he blew the horn. The familiar old man walking out of the office was none other than his old friend Wilbur Kettleman. He'd become a true family friend and an ally throughout the years. Nelson pulled the keys out of the ignition, pushed open the door with a grunt, and walked out toward him. The two old friends shook hands. Wilbur hadn't seemed to age in the years since, but then between the booze, the cigars, and the chewing tobacco, his age would probably be a tough guess to anyone who laid eyes on him.

"Come on in the office, Nelson. This Florida heat is murder on an old man like me."

"Florida heat? Man, you were born and raised here. You should be used to it by now."

"Skin's getting thin, Nelson. Skin's getting thin." He smiled.

Nelson followed him into the office: the old wooden shed of a cabin that had always served as his place of business and his home. He wasn't one for many renovations; he wanted his cabin retreat to take the visitor back to the 1950s. Wilbur sat on the old wooden stool, but Nelson stood near the window, glanced back at his car for a second then motioned for the padded stool on the counter.

"Okay—what's going on, Wilbur? What's all this stuff you were talking about on the phone? And it better be good." He pounded his finger on the counter with the last three words.

The old man's dentures were set in. An eighty-seven year old still doing what he loved to do was rare. Even though Florida was the land of retirees, Wilbur was the keeper of this peaceful vacation setting and called the cottages home. He raised his hand and waved a wagging finger at his guest.

"I know what you're going to say, Nelson, but I know what I saw, I know what Tobey McIntosh at the post office told me he saw, what Caroline Luna, the florist, said she saw, and what Colleen Hakan, the schoolteacher, told me she saw. These are good people Nelson, by God!"

"I know they are, Wilbur. Now, what happened?"

"Then you know Will Taylor, the pastor over at First Baptist? Why, he gave a message about the walking dead. I'm a God-fearin' man, Nelson! You know the prophet Ezekiel was in the land of the dry bones and he saw, uh wait, was that Ezekiel or was it Isaiah? Wait, I have a Bible over here somewhere…"

"Wilbur!"

Nelson slammed his fist against the counter, and Kettleman jumped.

"What did you see?"

"Well, tarnation, Nelson, I've been trying to tell you all along! Stop jabbering so I can tell ya, for crying' out loud. Some people just jibber-jabber all the time. I say if ya's got a point to make, then good googly-goop, just out and say it! Know what I mean?"

Nelson fidgeted his shaky palm and covered his face with both hands, exhaling a long, slow breath.

"Wilbur, can you please just…"

"Now, when I was talking to Colleen Hakan—wait. Have you met Colleen? She's a native of the Seminole tribe; she's the oldest school teacher in Old Indian Lake…"

Nelson started to bite his lip. "Wilburrrr…." He dragged the letter r.

"Okay, okay… stop interrupting so I can tell ya's. You ready for this? Cause if ya ain't I'm 'bouts ta tell ya anyway."

"Oh my God!" Nelson whispered to himself.

"I seen Sierra's family, standing at the water's edge right

over there, except they had these dark moles all over 'em, and they looked like zombies, well kinda like zombies. Not the kind you see in today's movies and TV. I'm talking about the old George Romero type—rest his soul! And they were standing right out there."

He pointed, and Nelson looked out the window. To his astonishment, he saw Sierra standing at the shore.

"Oh my God!" he sighed.

"What?" Wilbur asked. Then he also looked out. "Tarnation!"

Both men ran out to the lake. Sierra was standing there, hands to her face, crying and staring out at the water. This was exactly what Nelson hadn't wanted to happen.

It was calm and peaceful at the water's edge. The only sound to be heard, aside from Nelson's feet scrambling to get to her, was of the seagulls squawking overhead.

"Sierra! For Pete's sake! How did you get here!?"

She turned to him. In all the time he had purposefully kept her holed up in St. Petersburg and away from here, these brief few seconds brought back all the anguish, the pain, the loneliness she'd felt most of her life. It took only ten seconds, and she seemed like she was ready for a nervous breakdown. The look on her face broke his heart.

"Uncle Nelson…" she started crying, and he took her in his arms in a long hug.

"Sweetheart, I didn't want you to be here. Did you stow away in my car?"

She nodded her head; he turned to find his trunk open.

"Baby, I didn't want you to come. I didn't even want you to know that I was coming out here. This is bad for you…."

48

"Sierra, honey—uh, did you see anything out there?" Wilbur asked. He flanked her other side.

She pulled away from Nelson and smiled at the old man, then shook her head no. She took him in a hug.

"You know, I been thinking about you, Sierra. You been on my mind a lot lately. You doing okay, child? Been too long, had me worried. Nelson here don't know nothing about child rearin'"

"You don't either, Wilbur!" Nelson barked.

He ignored Nelson. "You doing all right, child?"

"Yes, Mr. Kettleman," she said with a forced smile.

He pulled a handkerchief from his overalls' front pocket, handed it to her.

"Well, welcome back to Old Indian Lake, the place of your birth."

She blew her nose, then wiped her eyes of drained tears, then turned to him. For an instant, Wilbur Kettleman saw the baby who was delivered right on these shores; then the ten-year-old he remembered the last time he had seen her, standing in the middle of the lake, and now she stood before him a young woman.

"Mr. Kettleman, may I ask you something?"

"Sure, girl, shoot."

"Well, when I was little, Mommy used to tell me the story about how I was born...."

Nelson rolled his eyes, brushed his hair back in a frustrated wave of his hand. Behind her back he drew a line across his neck to let Wilbur know that under no circumstances should he share the story. He already knew what was going to be coming next.

"She always told me that the only people that really knew were you and the old Indian man."

Nelson stepped between them, turning her so she faced him.

"Sierra, didn't we go over this? Your dad told me time and again that she had passed out after giving birth to you on the canoe. We have to believe him, honey; no one else saw it."

"That's not what Mommy told me, Uncle Nelson."

Wilbur took Nelson by the shoulder and shoved him aside, then stared into the girl's dark brown eyes.

"What did she tell you, sweetheart?" he asked.

She glared back solemnly at the water, then turned back to the old man.

"Mommy told me that she was wading in the water, then went swimming; then she felt the labor pains; then she started to drown… and then an old Indian man was on a canoe and saved her, in the middle of a thick fog, and he helped Mommy give birth to me right on the boat. She said he said some words… like only two words the whole time it happened."

"Two words?"

"Yeah when she told me, I wrote them down, then I looked it up a couple of years ago. It's Seminole, from the Seminole Indian tribe. It means 'little girl' and 'water.'"

"The old Seminole…" Wilbur said, rubbing his chin in deep thought.

It was clear that he was reminiscing, revisiting that fateful day in his mind, and it bothered him. He turned to approach the shoreline, walking away from them.

"Wilbur, does this actually mean something?"

The old man was silent; he stood gazing at the peaceful ripples. Nelson reached over and took his arm.

"Wilbur?"

He turned to the two. Sierra was staring at him.

"I have to know, Mr. Kettleman. Please…this has been haunting me all my life."

Wilbur's took on a dazed expression, like he was fighting what to say to her, though he knew she had to know the truth. But Nelson would have his head.

"I know it's been haunting you, child. I…yes, I remember that day. Your mother, she was so beautiful Sierra, just like you. She didn't listen to me or her husband to stay out of the water. I, uh… I didn't say anything to anybody."

"Say anything about what?" Nelson asked.

Wilbur stared back out at the calm water and dropped his head.

"I saw it… I saw what happened, I did. But I couldn't tell anyone. They'd think I was crazy. You understand, right?"

"What did you see?"

"I mean, you have to remember, I was here alone. And she was in the water – now who's gonna believe anything I say, even when she kept swearing she saw him, and she kept telling her husband, and nobody believed her, and I – I had to keep my mouth shut."

"Wilbur…"

"I wanted to say something, Sierra, I swear, but I just didn't have the nerve. I used to drink a lot back then, and people said I hallu, uh hallicita, uh, hallucit… that I made stuff up ."

"Wilbur…"

"How do you say you saw something that you know you saw but no one else saw except for the person it happened to, and no one believed her anyway, and they wouldn't believe what I said I saw, which was exactly what she saw? No one would believe it, right?"

"WILBUR!"

He jumped again.

"Mr. Kettleman, please, what did you see?" she took hold of his arms.

He looked out at the water and as he retold it to them, he saw it happen all over again in his mind, something he'd been trying to shake off for years.

"I saw her walk out to the water. She seemed like she needed to relax, you know? Her husband, the poor fella, Joe didn't know how to relax, and he was on her like a den mother, making sure she had what she needed, making sure her body temperature was right, that she had all of his phone numbers in case of emergency…I mean, the man wouldn't relent. You know what was funny about him? In all the years I'd come to know him, I don't think I ever heard him once call his wife by her name—Tina. He always had some endearment: Honeysuckle, Buttercup, Sugarplum, Snickerdoodle… heh, always made me smile."

"And..?" Nelson rolled his eyes impatiently.

"And… well, she waded out deep. I mean, she told me she was just going to walk out in the shallows. So I let it go. I was nervous for her already—being in her condition and all. But she went out farther, and farther—next thing I know, she's a-floatin' out there. I thought to myself, The poor girl's husband won't cut her a break, so I'm going to leave her alone. That's what I said to myself, clear as day. I started to make myself another cup o' coffee right at that moment…"

Oh my God. Nelson was biting his lip again.

"I saw her start to struggle. I mean, I figured she could swim. She told me that she could swim, so I had nothing to worry about, right? I mean, the first thing you find out from people when they check in here is two things: cash or credit, and can ya swim? If they say yes, then you don't have to worry about it, but if they say no, then you try to talk 'em out of going in. I usually use the alligator story. I ain't never seen a gator, but, you know, you mention that to tourists and they'll stay out, ya know? Well, personally I think there may be a gator in there—this is Florida and all—but…"

Nelson was rubbing the wrinkles on his forehead, pacing around the man, and about to burst. "And..?!"

"Will you let me tell my story? Man, this uncle of yours is one impatient man. Anyway, I had the TV on, but I heard her scream, so I was about to get up and get the raft and go out to help, but then I did a double-take when I looked out the window. A mist appeared out of nowhere. It came right out of the water. Then a canoe—I don't even know where the canoe came from because it didn't look like any of the ones I got here. I gets them from Sanford's Boats, you know – over on Central? You remember Fred Sanford on Central? He died from a heart attack you know…"

"Anyway?" Nelson sighed impatiently, staring down at the sand.

Wilbur rolled his eyes.

"Anyway, this canoe comes from out of nowhere, and the old Seminole was there. He stretched out his hand and pulled her in the boat. He didn't even speak. She was screaming for help. He laid her down in the boat, and in a few minutes, I heard your first screams, Sierra. He reached in the lake, poured some water on you, and raised his hands toward the sky, and…"

Wilbur Kettleman took in a large gulp, then turned away again.

"And… and what?" Sierra asked.

"And… he put you back in your mother's arms, and he said something to her, and then… well…"

"Well, what? Don't just stop mid-sentence, man!"

"Well, then he was gone."

"Gone? Like he dived in the lake?"

"No Nelson, like in gone. He just… just up and vanished. I stood there on the porch rubbing my eyes. I had just downed a half of Jim Beam… I wasn't sure if, you know, if you drink half a bottle of whiskey, you start seeing things. Then start asking yourself if you saw what you think you saw—know what I mean? You don't know if things are real or apparatus, uh, apparitus, uh appa… ghosts. One time I swear I saw Elvis standing out there, holding his guitar. Yeah plain as day, the King was right there where the palmetto plants are, see?" he pointed, "Well, then on another day…"

"Wilbur!"

"Huh?"

"The old Indian?"

"Oh, yeah… well, the canoe started coming to shore like it was being pushed or something. You know, like with

one o' them small motors that people attach to their little
boats? I was considering buying one myself, interestin'
contraptions…"

"Mr. Kettleman, the canoe?"

"Oh yeah—so when it hit the shore, I ran out and by
golly there you were, cutest thing I ever saw. I took you in
my arms, you were so beautiful, and your mom was just
passed out. Blood was all over the boat. I never saw that
much blood in my life. Good thing I didn't wanna throw up
at that moment, huh?"

"So!?" Nelson fumed, wanting, to hurry the story along.

"So I called the ambulance and I swore to myself that I
would never tell anyone anything, after that day, and I didn't,
because, well you know…"

Wilbur Kettleman, normally a man of many words,
stopped right there and looked sheepishly down to the
ground. He smacked his teeth, then rubbed the stubble on
his face, then hunched his shoulders looking back at Nelson.

"Mr. Kettleman, that's exactly what Mommy said
happened." She took his arm.

"Well it did, just like that, Sierra honey, I swear on a
stack of Bibles."

"Are you kidding me?" Nelson barked. "You want me to
believe that the ghost of an Indian appeared out of nowhere,
came up from the water in some supernatural mist, and
delivered Sierra in the water with no anesthesia, tools, a mid-
wife, nothing?"

"Yep."

"Okay, in the middle of the day, in the middle of this
lake, he mysteriously pushed the boat here to this shore—

and then he just pulled a David Blane and vanished into thin air? Come on, Wilbur!"

"Uh, yepo. And who the hell's David Blane?"

"He's a magician, and I'm sorry, Wilbur, but that's preposterous!"

"Nelson, I don't care what you believe! I saw it happen, and I stand by what I saw, uh…but I'll deny it if you tell anyone."

"I believe you, Mr. Kettleman." Sierra smiled.

"Well, the old Seminole, he's who the town and lake were named after. It was a town legend that people don't talk about anymore. Back in the 1800s the US Government forced the Seminoles out. Some stayed to fight, some swore vengeance, but the old Seminole here was a holy man and he said he would die here. His last battle was somewhere here near the lake, and he went down in a bloody fight. A lot of his tribe and family ended up in Oklahoma during the Trail of Tears, when Andrew Jackson fought them here. But the old Indian, he was proud, he was strong, and he would not leave his ancestral land.

"The original name of this place was Okahumkee. That's what the Seminoles called it. It means 'bad water'; they believed that this lake was cursed, that it kept the souls of the people who died in this region. After that last battle, this land lay untouched until the 1950s, when a developer saw the potential in a convention town. Eisenhower put the highway out there, and this became a stop. I was born and raised here. My granddad helped build the highway, my dad helped build the convention center, and my great-great-granddad fought Native Americans here. We used to call them 'Indians' back then, ya know? You know they were called Indians because when Columbus discovered America, he thought he had actually landed in India and…"

Nelson reached over covered Wilbur's mouth. Sierra turned to the water with longing eyes. Her birth, her origins lay in this body of water, but also the lifelong torment in her soul originated here. She let out a disheartened sigh.

Nelson, on the other hand, glared a look of disbelief. He had never wanted anyone to tell her the story that Tina insisted was true, much less have to hear it word for word from Wilbur.

"Sierra honey, I'm sorry," the old man started. "If I could do anything to change what happened back then… if I coulda talked her out of going out there the day you were born, or talk your papa out of taking all four of ya's out there so he could serenade ya's with his guitar, Lord knows I woulda dunnit."

The teen turned and gave him a reassuring smile.

"It's okay, Mr. Kettleman."

Then they heard the gurgle. It was deep out in the lake, but they heard it.

"What was that?"

"It looks like a wave is trying to form." Nelson pointed out at it.

Sierra stood at the water's edge, curiosity shining on her face. All her life, she'd felt drawn to water. It wasn't something she could easily explain to anyone, so she kept it locked in. The gurgle out there coincided with a gurgle she felt in the pit of her stomach. It happened at exactly the same moment.

Bubbles rose to the top of the lake's surface, almost like it was boiling at the bottom center of the bed of water. Then they saw a disturbance. At first it looked like rain—except it was falling up from the lake. Then they saw fish jumping wildly about.

"What the—?"

The fish started heading toward the shore, skipping through the water in a frenzy. First the ripples that turned to waves were coming, then the fish right behind it—almost like something was disturbing them. They were jumping out of the water before the wave, and it was all headed right for where these three were standing.

"Oh no, not again!" Wilbur screamed.

He grabbed Sierra's arm and pulled her to run toward the cottage, but she yanked away from him. Nelson stood in shock. The fish were leaping out of the water—a fisherman's dream, and Nelson liked to fish. But as exciting as this was, he could sense the imminent danger. The wave grew bigger and got closer. He had to move. The rushing sound of the wave was unheard of for a still lake like this. It was the kind of wave he was used to seeing from his window while glaring out at the beach back home as the warm waters of the Gulf of Mexico would come crashing down on the shore, the kind of waves that amateur surfers look for. But this wasn't the Gulf. This wasn't St. Pete Beach, and for some reason the wave coming toward them seemed to be filled with a life source that was totally alien to him.

"Sierra! Let's go!" Nelson screamed, grabbing her hand.

He tugged at her forcefully, but she yanked her palm

out of his demanding grip, and he fell away, rolling to the dirt behind the car. He reached up and hurriedly slammed his trunk closed. Sierra stood there watching the wave come dangerously ever closer to where she stood and showed no fear whatsoever.

"Sierra!"

He hopped to his feet to reach her, but it was too late. The threatening menace of a wave was right on her, towering about ten feet over her and daring to pummel her hard onto the ground. She closed her eyes and spread out her arms as the fierce, solid wall of water crashed down on the shore. But with all the force, rage, and speed of this impenetrable colliding mammoth of nature, it missed her. To the amazement of the two men witnessing this phenomenon, as it fell with a fury toward her, it opened into a hole right around Sierra and didn't touch her. But it did hit land, and it did so with a vengeance. The pounding thunderclap shook the ground around them, but the fifteen-year-old siren stood unfazed and dry.

Wilbur was knocked off his feet, lying on the ground against the cabin with his feet sticking up in the air as he gasped for breath. Nelson was drenched from head to toe; the wave had totally covered his car and shoved his face into the sand.

"Sierra!?" he screamed choking for air and wiping his dirt-filled face.

He struggled to his feet, slipped, and fell back down on his face. The mouthful of mud didn't help his mood. He got up and turned to his niece. She was still standing at the lake, looking peacefully out into the water. Wilbur ran to her and stood in front of her… but she stared blankly out into the lake, like he wasn't even there. He waved his hands in front of her eyes.

"Sierra honey, you okay?"

Nothing.

"She… she looks like she's in some kinda trance or something Nelson!"

Then he heard the wild flopping of the fish that had been thrust out on land. They were all over the place, slapping the sand in their frenzied dance.

"Whoo doggy!" the old man yelped.

Wilbur ran off toward the cabin, rushed back out with a wheelbarrow, and started throwing them in. Nelson looked over at him in shock.

"Whenever this happens, I get free fish. I sell them to Donny's Market, up the road." He smiled, showing his stained dentures, "You remember Donny? He used to be the chef at Hookahi's—man, that was a great place till the health department closed them down. Now he's running the fish market up the corner on Page Street and… Nelson, get to your girl now. Bring her to the cabin. Hurry!"

"This happens a lot?" Nelson asked, rushing to Sierra.

"Yup."

Nelson stood in disbelief, dripping wet and watching Wilbur Kettleman throw fish into the wheelbarrow while humming a song to himself; then he turned back to where Sierra was standing. She stood firm, glaring out at the water.

He ran up to her. "Honey, are you…?"

"Shhh!" she commanded.

"Sierra…." She heard it. It was faint, like a whisper, but

it came from out in the water.

Nelson leaned down to take a deep breath. His ribs were aching, and he started wiping water and mud from his shirt and pants and skin.

"Man what was that, a tsunami?" he asked, reaching out to Sierra. "Honey, I don't know how you got spared, but I sure am thankful. You could have gotten killed and…."

She broke away. Something had caught her full attention, and he couldn't break her from her gaze.

"Sierra honey?" He watched her take her first step into the water.

"Sierra, no!"

"Sierra, come…" the voice said.

She walked out onto the water.

"Sierra, don't! What are you doing?" he yelled.

Then he stepped back in astonishment. It wasn't the fact that she was walking out to the water that shocked Nelson and now Wilbur, who dropped the fish he was holding in his hand. It was the fact that she was walking on the water. She never sank as she walked in. She gradually strolled out on top of the rippled surface, taking the same kind of steps one would while stepping on beach sand.

"Sierra?" Nelson stood at the shoreline with a look of pure puzzlement, scratching his head.

"Look, look out there!" Wilbur pointed.

Nelson followed his shaking finger and saw forms slowly taking shape out on the water.

He squinted, trying to focus hard while he inched closer to the water to reach for his niece.

"What is… wait, Joe? Tina? The baby… what… what the

hell's going on here, Wilbur? Wait a minute, Sierra, don't go out there!"

Sierra's family appeared more discernible. They were standing on the water out in the middle of the lake.

"See? Ya see? I told you!" Wilbur smirked nervously, slapping his wet overalls, "Yeah, sure, who's going to believe old Wilbur Kettleman, the crazy drunk? The lonely widower who's half out of his mind? Huh? Well, do you believe me now, huh, Nelson?"

"No, Sierra, don't go out there! Please!" Nelson screamed again.

He ran through the shallows and jumped into the water, and started swimming toward her. He got out twenty feet from the shore and then quickly realized his new dilemma. Though he was stroking as hard as he could, he wasn't moving anywhere; then the water around him started to form into a whirlpool, and he was caught in it.

"What the..?"

He was a good swimmer, and he knew it, but the pressure of the spinning caused him to sink into the middle of it. It was a gradual rush of swirling water that seemed to originate right under him.

"Nelson!?" Wilbur called.

The older gent ran to the shore, looked around for something to help—a rope, a branch—something.

"Hang on, buddy, I'll help ya!" He ran back to the shed to get rope.

Sierra kept her eyes out front, staring at her family.

"Sierra, come…"

"Madre de Dios! Sierra!" Nelson screamed.

She jerked from his cry, and it seemed to hurt—pulling herself away from the force that was drawing her to the center of the lake and then hearing Nelson's scream. She turned her head and saw Nelson sinking into the whirlpool. Her eyes widened in fright, but then curled into a frown. Though the force out in the lake was strong, she had to help her uncle.

"No!" she screamed.

Then the whirlpool turned inside-out as she raised her hand, and he was lifted to his feet in the water by the upside-down whirlpool. It gradually pushed him back safely to the shore.

"Sierra… what is going on here?" Nelson asked. "Please don't go out there!"

He landed on the sand in a hard thump next to a bewildered Wilbur Kettleman, who was holding tattered rope in his grip. Seeing him safely on the shore, she turned back to fix her view on her family, and saw that they had started to sink back into the water. "Daddy? Mommy? No!"

As she ran toward them on the water with all her might, the tears started to flow.

"Daddy!?"

Wilbur and Nelson stood staring at this, and Nelson's stomach started churning again. He held it, patted it down.

"Oh man—I've gotta go. This is a bad time, Wilbur!"

"Where?"

"Bathroom, now!" he ran back toward the cabin, "No, no, no! I can't hold it! Do something, Wilbur. Save my niece!"

He ran into the cottage office. Sierra was still barreling

across the now-smooth surface toward her family, and they began to sink into the deep coldness of Old Indian Lake.

Nelson ran into the bathroom, struggling to loosen his pants, and slammed the door. Meanwhile, Wilbur walked out to the water's edge. "Sierra honey," he called, "maybe you shouldn't go out there! You wanna go out for some ice cream or somethin'?"

He was twirling the rope to no avail, thinking he could reach her. She stopped on the water where her family had sunk, turned to the old man.

"Mr. Kettleman, they're going away again! What do I do?" she cried.

They locked eyes for a few seconds; then she looked down at the water again. The last ripple told her they were gone. "Daddy?"

A mist slowly started out of nowhere, seeming to build from the water itself, and was soon covering her. This was familiar to the older gentleman; he'd seen the same thing happen the day Sierra was born and countless mornings afterward, almost like it was looking for her to come back. And finally here she was, back at the very spot where it all had happened fifteen years ago. Wilbur ran to the shed, dragged out his little rowboat, threw the rope in, hopped in, and started rowing out into the water. He didn't know what was going on, but he felt a duty to save this girl.

"Sierra, for God's sake!" he screamed, "Stay right where you're at. I'm a-comin'! Don't be scared!"

He rowed hard.

"Don't be scared," he said mocking himself. "I'm about to loosen my bowels in my britches right here in this boat."

Sierra turned, glancing around in quick jerks of her head inside the mist.

From where Wilbur was, rowing as fast as he could, he could see the mist creepily enveloping her till she was almost out of plain sight.

"Oh Lord, something's gonna happen to that girl if I don't get there in time!"

Sierra stood still and saw a canoe appear right next to her, and inside was the old Seminole. He smiled calmly. She looked at him. She knew she should have been afraid, but she wasn't. He wasn't going to hurt her. For some reason, she knew this. He stretched out his hand to her in a welcoming gesture.

"Chackshosti," he said in an old, worn voice.

"Chak… chackshosti?"

Wilbur was getting closer to the mist, Sierra didn't see him, but she did see, right next to her, ripples start again, and then a head rose out of the water. It was her little sister.

"Breanna? Oh my God, Breanna!" she smiled.

The old man reached out and put his hand on Breanna's head.

"Chackshosti."

"What does that mean? Sister?"

"No, it means daughter." Her little sister smiled.

Sierra stared at her; she was still the same age she had been when she went into the water that fateful day. A tear slowly formed in her eyes.

"Breanna – are you okay?"

Her little sister's face was full of dark splotches. He bent down to touch her, but Breanna backed away and held on to the canoe.

"I'm not really here, Sierra." She smiled.

"What do you mean, you're not here? I can see you…I can touch you, can't I?"

"Yeah, Sierra, but I'm not really here—well, not the way you see me, anyway. It's hard to explain. Wow, look at you. You're all growned up."

"I've missed you, and Mommy—and Daddy—so much."

"I know. We miss you too."

"Breanna, why does he call me 'daughter'?"

He stretched out his hand to her.

"Come with us, Sierra," she said.

"Come where?"

"Home."

"Where's home?"

He put his hand on Breanna's head again, tapping her.

"Is-tah-chee."

"Huh?"

"He said 'little girl'. He's the one who delivered you on the boat with Mom, Sierra. He's taken us home. We belong here. He wants you to come home with us. You have to."

"Why? Breanna, I miss you, but I don't want to die."

"But, it's the only way we can be together again, Sissi. We're not whole unless you're here. Besides, there's a battle coming. We need you."

"Huh? What are you talking about?"

The old Seminole waved at her to come. Breanna and he began to sink back into the water, canoe and all.

"Breanna, I'm not going down there!"

Her little sister kept staring at her as she sank into the

depths of Old Indian Lake.

"Breanna, please don't leave! Breanna!"

"Sierra!"

It was Mr. Kettleman; he had finally rowed his way to where she was and was cutting through the mist.

"Mr. Kettleman, go back."

"Not without you, Sierra. Tarnation, I don't know what's gotten into these waters lately, but we needs to get you back to shore. Now come on, girl. I don't wanna be out here any longer than I hafta!"

Suddenly the water started to boil, and ripples formed around where Sierra was standing.

"Uh, Sierra?"

"Go, Mr. Kettleman, now!" She pointed. "I don't think I can control it!"

"I can't leave you out here… and uh… how are you doing that—standing on the water like that there? That's kinda weird."

A wave churned and started pushing the small boat back to the shore. Inside the cabin, Nelson had just finished flushing the toilet and reached for the doorknob. He was just about to walk out the door when he heard the rumble behind him. He turned back to the toilet and it started shaking on the floor, and the water inside, instead of flushing back down, started to roar, and it turned into a furious whirlpool that rose out of the bottom of the commode.

"What the..?"

CRASH!

The toilet burst in half, and water flew all over the bathroom, drenching him again as he ran out the door.

"Wilbur!! Wilbuuur!?"

He hopped out of the front door and saw Wilbur on the boat, holding on for dear life and being whisked to the shore by a small tidal wave. "Oh no!" Wilbur screamed. "I'm too old for this. I'm too old for this!"

"Wilbur?"

The boat crashed onto the shore, and Wilbur rolled over on the sand, tangled in the rope and gasping in excitement. The old man landed at Nelson's feet. He looked out into the water; the mist had dissipated, and Sierra was sinking into the lake.

"Sierra, no!!" Nelson screamed. Although he had never had kids of his own, since raising Sierra from age ten, he knew the fears of a father. Watching her sink into this mysterious lake just didn't seem like something he'd want to have to remember years from now. He stepped to the shore, and suddenly a rushing wave formed in the shape of a hand, forcing him to stay where he was.

He kicked at the huge hand, punched at it, and attempted to run around it or dive through it, only to be pushed back on the beach. He landed next to Wilbur, who was trying to untangle himself from the rope. Glaring back out into the lake, he could see his worst fear materialize.

The mist was gone.

And so was Sierra.

CHAPTER SEVEN

The mysteries of the deep are a fascinating subject for many a marine biologist and diver, and anyone connected to water. We long to know what's down there. Sometimes, though, it might be better not to know. Sierra was about the find out. She opened her eyes. She knew she had gone down under the lake, but she didn't feel wet. This actually felt like a scene from several of her nightmares, so although it was scary, it was oddly familiar to her.

"Where am I?"

It took a few seconds to focus, and when she did, the

first thing she saw was a pair of red eyes staring at her.

"No… I'm dreaming again. I'm dreaming again!"

The red eyes slowly darkened to brown as they got closer, and a form emerged from the darkness. Then she recognized the face of the person floating in front of her.

"Mom!?"

"Sierra." she smiled.

"Mom? Is this… real? I'm dead, aren't I?"

"No, honey, you are not dead." She smiled.

Though she was underwater, she could feel the tears swell. The sight of her long-lost mother, right in front of her, floating with the finesse of a mermaid, caused her to want to break down.

"How did I…what's going on?"

"Honey, we need you. This is important." Her mother's beautiful face had never changed from the beauty of years past. She seemed to never age.

"Huh? You guys keep saying you need me. Need me for what? Can't we just be a family again? I mean, I love Uncle Nelson, but I miss you."

Her mother pointed to the old Seminole, who stood beside her. They were floating underwater in the middle of the lake; Sierra could hear Nelson and Wilbur screaming her name from the surface.

"Running Deer is a medicine man. He was put here to protect the region. When they forced his people to leave, he stayed. He says he knew this moment would come; it was destiny. This land is sacred to his people. We need to keep it safe. Sierra honey, you need to keep it safe."

"Safe? Safe from what?"

"Come with us. We will show you."

Sierra looked around. Her dad and little sister were right behind her. The Seminole reached out again. She struggled inside for a decision. If I touch him, I may never go back up… but I want to be with Mom and Dad. Is this how it ends? I die underwater like in my dreams?

Finally the troubled teen gave in and decided to take the hand of the mysterious stranger who had haunted her for most of her life and who was now here, right in front of her. Their hands connected as if in slow motion, and she looked at him. His smile was reassuring, but as soon as they touched, she passed out.

Up on the shore, the two men were screaming her name but were prevented from wading out into the water by the almost human-looking hand created by the wave that kept threatening to push them back. Nelson had never seen anything like it, but Wilbur wasn't surprised. Having been a native of Old Indian Lake, Florida, he was used to weird happenings, and this was kind of normal to him. Still, it gave him a chill.

"What are we going to do, Nelson? She could be drowning!"

"No, no! She's a good swimmer. I taught her to hold her breath. She can hold her breath longer than anyone. She's just lost down there, Wilbur. She'll make it. Come on, Sierra."

He was reassuring the old man but really trying to pacify his own anxiety. He wanted to believe she was okay, but he would never be sure unless he checked himself, and he had to know.

"I have to… have to get to my baby!"

Nelson jumped back into the water, through the hand, and this time he made it through.

"Sierra!"

He dived in and swam out, nothing stopping him this time, but when he got to the spot where he knew she had submerged, she was no longer there. Frantic, he went under and looked around, holding his breath as much as he could, struggling under water for a sign, a clue, anything. Sierra was nowhere to be found. He finally surfaced after five failed attempts and looked back out at the shore.

"She's gone, Wilbur, she's gone! I promised him I would watch over her! I promised Joe! My…my baby…our baby! She's gone!"

For the last five years of Sierra's troubled life, Nelson had been father, mother, uncle, best friend, and big brother to her. He had raised her like he would have his own, and now, in a split second, she was gone, taken from him, and at that very moment Nelson Vargas knew the grief of the father of a lost or missing child. He treaded steadily, punching his fist into the water.

"Sierra! No, you can't do this! Give her back to me! She's just a baby! Sierra?"

Nelson cried alone in the depths of Old Indian Lake.

Back at the shore, Wilbur drew a cross in the sand with his feet.

"Bless her soul. Bless you, Sierra."

CHAPTER EIGHT

"Sierra?"

She twitched when she heard her name. The male voice
sounded familiar, but she knew it wasn't Nelson or Wilbur,
the only two voices that common sense told her she should
be hearing. Slowly her eyes opened, and she looked around.
She was in a cave. It was a dark, damp crevice of a room
that smelled of fish and mold. The walls, if that's what they
were, were wet, had splotches of holes all about, green algae
creeping out of them and some other plant she had never
seen before. She rubbed her eyes. She was still dripping wet,

but she wasn't under water anymore.

"Nelson? Mom? Daddy? Bree?"

She slowly sat up on the stone slab, wiped her eyes, and tried to focus around the room. She saw a figure slowly approaching from her right, but her vision was still blurred.

"Daddy?"

"No, Sierra my child, it is I, Running Deer. We finally meet again, though not on the best of terms."

She was fully seated now, and the old Native American medicine man approached her and stood at her side with a solemn look that made him look more like a statue than a person. But then again, she wasn't even sure that she was actually in the presence of a person or…

"Are you a ghost? And why are you speaking English now?"

He stretched out his hand and waved back her wet hair.

"I am with you in essence, and I am speaking my native tongue, but you understand me, do you not?"

She looked up into his stone-cold, dark eyes. He seemed to stare right through her and didn't offer a grin or any facial expression of any kind. His stoic stance almost demanded respect, like a priest or dignitary would. All her life he was that man in the dreams, but there he was, talking with her. He stood taller than she expected, and his skin had a bright reddish brown tone. Though light was scarce, he seemed to almost glow. The top of his head was wrapped lightly in a thin, shiny cloth, and several large feathers adorned the back. Beads hung off his neck, and his left shoulder was covered in a fur-type shawl that her sight became glued to.

"Yes I–I do understand you. But how? And where are

Mom and Dad? Where's my little sister?"

"They–they are not able to be with you at present." He turned and looked at a crevice in the cave wall behind him.

"Well, where are they?"

"Sierra, I had to make you think you saw them. They were spirits. It was the only way I could make you come. I have long been trying to bring you back home for all of your life. Your family is safe, they are with the spirits. But for the past five years I have called you, I have sought you."

She rubbed her head again, squinted almost like from a slight headache.

"I–I know; I could actually feel that. All those years I could feel you, but I ignored it, I ignored you because…."

"Because you did not want your guardian to think you were suffering from lunacy. Truly, you are not losing your senses, young Sierra Nora Russo."

The last time she had heard her full name was when she was ten, and it was her mother who called her that every time she wanted to get her attention. She looked around in the damp cavern, which seemed to have halls coming from every direction.

"Why do I have this weird power over water? What did you do to me when I was born? Is this why you keep haunting me?"

She turned on the stone table so that her legs were hanging off the side. She didn't feel she was ready to stand yet. Though she could feel that she wasn't hurt in any way, she felt a slight throbbing on her right temple, it made her a little dizzy.

"Legend says that once in 5000 seasons, a child will be born on the waters of Okahumkee."

"Bad water… that's what your people call the lake."

He nodded in agreement with her.

"I was once that child… you were the next. Your body and water are one. Your skin, your hair, your organs were bonded with the natural surroundings of this 'bad water.' It is your fate. You are special, Sierra. You are to be revered among your kind, but you will be feared among your kind – as I was. They made me a holy man because of the gifts bestowed on me, but I was a warrior first. Our people, our home must never be relinquished. It must stay with our people. The spirits so command it."

"What are you talking about?"

"Your birth here was not by chance, my daughter."

"Why do you keep calling me your daughter? And what happened to Mom and Dad, and Breanna? They really… died?"

He stepped closer to her, took her hand.

"You ask many questions. They are with the spirits, my child. I am sorry. But you have a purpose here. Come…"

"No!" she cried yanking her hand back.

She hopped off the slab and dropped to her knees. The dizziness in her head wasn't quite gone. He reached down to help her up.

"No!"

She pulled back and leaned against the slab. As she looked around again, there was only a small hint of light coming from the left side of the cave. She pulled herself up, then tried to find a way out. Every step she took echoed off a puddle of water under her in the dark-creviced cavern. It smelled like water, felt like water, but she knew she wasn't under water anymore. She glared around in frustration. All the caverns at her disposal, and she had no idea how to get out—or where, for that matter, 'out' was.

"I saw them! I wanted my family to still be alive. How could you, how could you fool me like that? Do you know how cruel that is?"

"Sierra, there is an injustice coming. You are my only hope. You have to do this for me, for my people, for our home…"

"Do what?! You tricked me into thinking my family was still here. I had my own hopes. I could have gone off with them and been happy. How could you do that? What kind of a person are you? Even if they're dead and you have the power to bring them back, then why wouldn't you do that knowing the pain I have suffered all my freaking life?"

"I am very sorry for the deception, but you see, Sierra, this is important."

"I'm not helping you!" she screamed, pointing at him.

She turned and ran for the light and tripped on something that moved right in front of her. Tumbling on the rocky floor, she rolled over to see what it was.

"Growwwwl!"

"An—an alligator!" she screamed.

It turned on her and opened its huge mouth, showing off its ferocious teeth.

"Halputta, waugus cheh!" Running Deer commanded.

Sierra rolled over and hopped to her feet.

"Alligator, lie down," she whispered to herself, repeating

what he had just said. "Then Mr. Kettleman was right. There is an alligator."

"Halputta will not harm you, nor anyone on the shore. She guards the cave. Daughter, please stay?"

She glared at the alligator, moving her hand to the left. Its head followed, and then to the right; it did the same. But the alligator would not move from where she stood; it seemed like Running Deer had an invisible leash on the animal.

"Sierra, you must listen."

"No!"

She ran for the opening, stopped, and turned back to him.

"I'm going back to Uncle Nelson, I'm leaving this place! Forever! I'm going back to St. Petersburg!"

He stood silent, slowly frowned. She stomped her foot on the wet ground and stormed out, running for the light at the cave door. He sighed and looked into the crevice of the cave to his right, and Tina Russo walked out.

"Running Deer, she'll come back. Deep inside, I know that she wants to help. She just doesn't feel the urgency yet." her mother said. She bent down to pet the alligator.

He nodded in worried agreement, then faced the open cave door. They could hear her footsteps as she ran farther and farther away.

"I know, but she is right Tina—I should not have deceived her. For that I am eternally shamed. She is stubborn, but she is my only hope."

Back at the shack, Wilbur tried hard, but he couldn't calm Nelson down.

"The sheriff is coming with the dive team. They'll be here any minute. Don't go back in, Nelson. You won't find her."

"Wilbur, I gave Joe my word! I swore on his empty grave that I wouldn't let any harm come to her! I did my best to keep her away from here. Why did she have to stow away in my car! Why?"

He replayed in his mind the funeral—a funeral that was actually more ceremony than traditional funeral because the bodies of the Russo family were never recovered. They vanished into the abyss of Old Indian Lake. But he felt he owed a duty to his friend, and to Sierra. So he buried three empty caskets in their names. He reflected on that unforgettable moment, standing at Joe's grave, tears filling his eyes and not knowing a thing to say to his dead friend except, "I promise you, Joe, with every hair on my head, I will protect your daughter. I will watch her like she's my own. I won't let any harm come to her. I give you my word, buddy, partner, compadre. Te lo juro... I swear it."

"I promised, I swore to him that I would watch his baby. I put my life on hold for her. Don't you see Wilbur?"

"I do, Nelson. I do see. And a sacrifice like that won't go unnoticed, but I'm tellin' ya, jumping back in the water ain't going to do you a bit of good. Hell, you may end up with your old partner, and what good is that gonna do that poor girl? If she made it, she'll come up on another side of the lake. There's a spring over there." He pointed. "But if she drowned, she could be washing up on any side of the lake." He gulped. "Or worse."

"Worse? What could be worse than that!?" Nelson screamed, punching the wall.

"He means the gator," said a deep voice at the door.

Nelson turned. There were two older teens with scuba tanks and flippers and a uniformed gentleman standing right in the doorway. It was his baritone voice that Nelson had heard.

"Gator? I thought you said you were kidding about the gator when you talked to Tina?"

"Come on, Nelson. We live in Florida. Gators are like the state pet here. You know better than that. Now, that right there's a fresh water lake. You know there's gotta be gators in there. That's why I don't go in, 'cept on my boat to fish."

Nelson turned to the sheriff at the door, then turned back to Wilbur as tears started to stream again. After a deep exhale and a swipe of his nervous hand across his forehead, he pointed out at the water.

"Wilbur, have you actually seen a gator in the water?"

"Ha, you know, Tina asked me the same thing fifteen years ago." Wilbur smiled.

"And your answer was…?"

"Well, no, I ain't seen no gators, but…."

"Then how can you come to that conclusion? Anyone ever been killed by a gator in this lake?"

Nelson looked around; none of the four men standing there said anything. The two teens shrugged their shoulders.

The sheriff walked in and put his hand on Nelson's shoulder. "Mister, you from around here?"

Nelson shook his head. The other two just stared, showing no kind of emotion whatsoever.

"He's from St. Pete, Jeb." Wilbur coughed

"Oh, big city boy, eh?"

The two young men in scuba gear chuckled to themselves, elbowing each other.

Nelson spoke up. "Uh, excuse me—are you guys going in to look for Sierra, or would you like to lend me a set of your frog feet? Time's wasting here!"

The sheriff stared at Nelson. His graying hair and olive complexion set him apart in the eyes of the lawman; there weren't many Hispanics in Old Indian Lake, but he understood the rush. He twisted his moustache and turned to the two frogmen.

"Chris, Tyler. Go on; find the girl. This may take us the rest of the day, but you know what to do."

"Yes sir." Chris, the younger of the two, smiled.

The two brothers were the best swimmers in Old Indian Lake, and they knew this body of water better than almost anyone. Both were fit, with thin, athletic bodies, and could almost have passed as twins, with the same short blond hair, blue eyes, and sharp smile. Only two years separated them in age.

Chris, the fifteen-year-old, approached the water first. "Come on, Ty. Let's do it."

"Now we're getting somewhere," Nelson fumed.

"Wilbur, you got any coffee on?" the lawman asked.

"Na, but let me go and make ya a quick cup. I bought me one of them there Keurig contraptions. I had 'em in the cabins and finally got myself one. I don't know, Jeb. It just don't taste the same to me. Know what I mean? I miss the old percolator myself. Ha, I mean just yesterday I was gonna…"

"Uh, Sheriff?" called Tyler from outside.

The lawman turned to the open door and stepped out on the porch, Nelson looked out too, and Wilbur was coming up close behind. The three men congregated on the small wooden porch after being shoved out by Wilbur, and their jaws dropped when they saw the ripple in the water. Something was headed toward the shore. Whatever it was it was underwater and coming straight toward where the two divers stood.

"Y'all step away now, step away from the shoreline!" the deep, husky voice with the Southern twang commanded.

He reached down and loosened the gun out of its holster.

"Uh, gator?" Wilbur asked.

"No, you'd see the head and tail if it were."

Chris called back, "Whatever it is, it's moving fast. I wish I could move that quick underwater."

Nelson stepped off the porch and started walking out toward the two young brothers.

"Nelson, now don't go doing nothing stupid, boy!" Wilbur said, leaning back on the doorframe.

They saw the ripples get closer, closer, then hair, then a head, then… a face.

"Sierra!" Nelson screamed.

He ran toward the shore and past the two brothers into the water. Sierra walked out of the water and into Nelson's nervous embrace.

"Sierra honey, are you okay? Tell me you're okay! Come on. Let's get in the car. I'm taking you to the hospital just to make sure."

"No, I'm okay, Uncle Nelson," she mumbled.

The two brothers took notice of the young woman walking out of the water. To Nelson, who had raised her, and had always looked on her as a daughter, she was the light of his eyes, but for the first time he saw what they saw: a young woman. Sierra was a beautiful, dark, serious yet dazed young woman, with looks that could stop traffic. Something about her had changed; it was like she had aged while she was gone those few minutes.

Wilbur gave her a quick hug.

"Lordy be, Sierra, you had us going there. What with seeing mirages on the water of your family and all…"

"I… I want to go home, Uncle Nelson."

"Sierra… stay.…"

They all heard it this time. It was almost like the wind had spoken, and it was unnerving to the ear. The quick breeze over the surface of the cool lake brought a chill to all who were there—all except Sierra. That chill felt natural to her now. She knew, whether she liked it or not, that she was one with this region. The two brothers turned around to the water but saw nothing. The sheriff had his gun drawn and aimed out into the lake. He looked at Wilbur, who smirked, smacking his teeth.

"Voices coming from the water. That ain't nothing new. I'm going back in to make coffee. Still want some, Sheriff? I got Donut Shop, Blueberry, Caribou, Morning Blend, Dark Roast…" he kept calling them out as the screen door slammed behind him.

"Come on, Sierra. I'm taking you home." Nelson smiled, holding her in his arms. The two brothers walked behind them.

"Uh, excuse me," Chris said, tapping her on the shoulder. "Uh, what did you see down there?"

Nelson and Sierra stopped; she turned to them and tried not to look out at the water. Tyler walked up to her.

"Why?" she asked. She sized Tyler up and down in a quick visual glance. Sierra was five-foot six, so he had to be at least five-nine with a thin, muscular build, same as his younger brother.

"You see, Sierra, we hear about a lot of strange stuff out there, but no one but Wilbur ever sees it, so the town kinda thinks he's, well you know…lost it." He smiled.

"I heard that!" Wilbur screamed from the window.

She looked at seventeen-year-old Tyler, his clean-shaven face, military-style crew cut, and muscular arms with a tattoo on his right bicep that read 'Mom-Mom.' Chris was almost his twin, just about half an inch shorter, and a shark fin necklace hung across his chest.

A slow smile crept over her face as water still dripped from her long hair. "Wilbur definitely has not lost it. What he says he hears is real."

"I saw it myself, guys," Nelson said.

"What did you see, sir?" Chris asked, stepping closer.

"Why is this important to you guys?" Nelson asked.

"I'm in college, marine biology," Tyler said. "This lake and its history are the subject of an essay I'm doing about urban beliefs and customs. Town rumor says this might have been the fountain of youth that Ponce De Leon was looking for, then there's rumors about this being the sacrificial lake of past druids who lived here, or the dwelling place of a certain family of the Seminole tribe. Either way, there's rich history on this site, so honestly, anything you can tell us will help, but also being natives of this town, we just want to know. Some of the older townsfolk say they have seen and heard stuff that none of us have. They've been saying it for years."

"What kind of stuff?" Nelson asked.

"Well, depends on who you talk to, but everybody seems to agree on one thing: something about an old Seminole warrior."

Sierra turned to Nelson; they stared at each other, pondering the next thing to say, then turned back at the brothers. She wanted to say something but stopped herself from doing so. This was her secret; she didn't feel it was safe to share with anyone, especially someone she'd just met. Her eyes and Nelson's met once more; they both shook their heads, no. He took his arm from around her shoulder and reached in his pocket for the keys. They all heard the keys jingle in his hand; then Sierra's temple started pounding again, and she felt weak at the knees.

"Oh." She fell faint, and Tyler grabbed her just before she hit the dirt. He picked her up in his arms.

"Put her in my car, quick!" Nelson screamed.

His car rushed hurriedly off the property and down the road as a cool, lonely wind whispered over the lake.

CHAPTER NINE

The pounding inside her head gradually faded to a soft pulse—soft enough for her to try and open her eyes. She felt groggy, but she was finally slowly gathering her senses enough to try and wake up. Outside of room 215 at the Old Indian Lake Community Clinic, no one else knew the severity of what the beautiful girl lying alone on the bed had undergone. Though she had been born here, Sierra Nora Russo wasn't a name familiar to pretty much anyone.

Nelson had gone to the cafeteria to get coffee. After his sitting diligently by her side the whole time, watching, waiting for something, anything, she wouldn't budge. She didn't respond to the lullabies he'd hum to her, or the dry jokes he'd crack while she was under. She didn't flinch when he softly stroked her long, dark hair away from her face and talked to her like she was awake. But it would just happen to be his luck that she'd start to wake up just after the moment he had walked out.

"Oh…" she held her head. It was still throbbing. Sierra wasn't prone to headaches, but she knew what they felt like, and this was reminiscent of a soft headache that she remembered having after a serious ice cream binge.

"What? What happened… where am I?"

Waking up in a strange room is no welcome event, and Sierra surely didn't recognize the walls or bed. She looked around, squinting at light sources around her.

"You're at the clinic. Are you feeling okay?"

She heard the voice but didn't recognize it at first. Impatience got the better of her, and she struggled to get up but slipped on the bed.

"Whoa, go slow, sister," the voice said with a hint of smile.

She felt the firm grip on her arm. He sat her up on the bed, and she rubbed her eyes. Sierra wasn't used to hospitals. All her life living with Nelson, she had never gotten sick, not even a cold. Finally her eyes adjusted to the dimly lit room. It was one of the divers from before. She looked into his blue eyes. He looked like he could be related to Zac Efron.

"Hi, Tyler Philips, remember me? Back at the lake? The diver?"

"Yeah, college student, full of questions." She rubbed her head smiling.

He smiled back. Hers looked like a smile of pain to him, though she was really just trying to get her bearings. She turned; there was a pitcher of water next to a Styrofoam cup. He followed her eyes.

"You want some water?"

She reached her hand out to the pitcher. She wasn't close, but he was. But as her open hand reached to the liquid container, it tipped over by itself, and water splashed out and landed miraculously in the cup intact that he held in his grip.

"Whoa!" he jumped when it happened, like he thought the pitcher was going to fall over to the floor and splash the water on him and all over the tiled floor. It didn't, it stopped when the cup was full.

"Wha…how did that happen? That was amazing, man we shoulda been taping that; we coulda made it on that show Funniest Home Videos or something." He reached over to her and placed the cup in her hands. She smiled, bringing it to her lips while never losing sight of the handsome teen. Nelson entered the door as she took her first sip.

"Sierra!" he grabbed her in a hug and hit the cup and the water ended up spilling all over Tyler anyway. He jumped from the splash of cold water on his shirt. "Aw, man!"

She giggled.

"Honey, are you okay?"

He held her by both arms, staring into her dazed face.

"Wow, your dad was so worried. He really loves you, Sierra."

"He–he's not my Dad…well," she had to clear her throat, then smiled and turned to Nelson, kissed him on the cheek. "I guess in a way, he is. Yeah he's my dad."

Nelson had never heard those words from her, and it brought a bright, warm smile to his worried face. The approaching nurse broke the conversation short as she made her way in. Hurried but calm, she put the back of her palm on Sierra's forehead, then looked at the chart.

"I think you're good to go Miss Russo." She turned to Nelson. "She's fatigued. Just get rest; you seem to have too many things overworking that beautiful head of yours. You're not old enough to be this tired young lady, no indeed." She waved her finger at her.

The nurse had the kind of smile that would force a smile out of anyone, and it worked on her. Sierra looked at her name tag, "Marjeanette."

"Wow I have never heard that name before… Marjeanette. That's pretty."

"Yes." The older African-American woman smiled. "My mother sure thought so. Now, you get home and please get some sleep. If I see you back here, I'm going to give you a job. In fact, they are going to be tearing down this old clinic and building a new hospital on the grounds. Yes ma'am, lots of changes coming to this town. I'll put in a good word for you, yes indeed."

"Uh, I'm not looking for a job."

"Why sure you are. Young girl like you needs to start somewhere. Go to school and get a part-time job here. I'll put in a good word for you. You're such a pretty little girl. Now go on home and get some much needed rest."

Marjeanette patted her on the back, then walked out humming to herself.

"I think the lady's right. You could get a job here and become a nurse just like her. Miss Marjeanette knows everybody. She could get you a job like this." He snapped his finger.

"I'm not feelin' it." Sierra shrugged.

"Well, she's also right that you need to get out of the clinic and get some rest." Tyler smiled. "I live with my grandma on the other side of the lake, and we have an extra room you can use."

"That won't be necessary, young man, but I appreciate your hospitality," Nelson interrupted. He placed his empty coffee cup in the teen's hand.

"Are we going back home, Uncle Nelson?" Sierra asked.

"Is that what you want?"

She thought for a little bit, remembering the faces of her sister, her father, and her mother, and that weird feeling of being underwater yet not drowning. Then the image of Running Deer crept in. She was upset at what had happened, but she wondered, why did he say that he needed her? Maybe there was something really going on? Something pressing that she might be able to actually help with? Though she had no idea what she could possibly do. Maybe there actually was some type of emergency, but what did he mean—he needed her help? He had an entire town and a sheriff's department he could go to.

She sat curiously thinking about it but then remembered how he had tricked her. He had her thinking that her family was still alive. She had actually seen them, spoken with them—and the fact that she could once again reunite with her family was what made him accessible to her, and that hurt. It hurt to the core. That sealed her decision in a split second. No she didn't want to stay. Why should she help a man who had lied to her? She frowned, thinking about it.

"Sierra?"

"Yes, Uncle Nelson. I think I want to go home."

"Aw man." Tyler grimaced. "I was kinda hoping you'd hang around."

"Sorry, but I really just need to get away from here. I want to be home."

CHAPTER TEN

Home. She would never have thought that seeing St. Petersburg Beach would be such a welcome sight, but she was so happy to be there. Nelson came in behind her, lugging his still-soaked bags. The meeting he'd hoped to have had never taken place, something he knew meant another trip very soon, but he had to do it, so he would, as soon as they called. The probable outcome would be too lucrative to skip the meeting and not go back.

Sierra went to the couch, exhaled a long, exasperated sigh, and allowed her weight to drop her on the plush piece of furniture. The roomy condo that Nelson had on the beach was decorated the way a man would decorate: framed posters, a fake plant here and there, a huge-screen TV attached to the wall, autographed baseball memorabilia, and not much else. But he kept a clean home, which Sierra helped with. It was a spacious three-bedroom with all modern everything, and he had turned the third bedroom into an office he could use for work if he needed to.

He rarely entertained guests or even had a social life. The one woman he did manage to almost have a serious relationship with didn't like the fact that he willingly sacrificed so much for the troubled teen. She had plans of her own on what to do—like sending Sierra to Palm Academy in DeLeon Beach. True, it was a great school, but it was also a good three-hour drive from St. Pete. That helped make it a very easy decision for him about which girl needed to go packing. He'd dedicated most of his time to raising Sierra, and he wasn't about to let someone else tell him how to do it. Between Sierra and his work, he didn't have time for anything else but TV and an occasional baseball game at Tropicana Field.

There was a knock at the door that quickly alerted Sierra that company had arrived. But she and Nelson had just walked in. Whoever it was had to have been walking right behind them.

Who could possibly..?

Nelson had just closed the bathroom door when she heard the knock, so Sierra walked over to the door and turned the knob. "Yes?"

The girl standing at the door wore an impatient glare that almost immediately annoyed Sierra.

"Brooke? Hi, uh…"

"So you don't wanna come to my party? What is it with you, Sierra? You don't answer your texts, I never see you on Facebook anymore, and do you even Snapchat? Girl what's up with you?"

Brooke, the voluptuous blonde who seemed to always be in competition with Sierra at school for everything, looked peeved. "Joey said you weren't even interested in my party. Did you even bother to know who was coming?"

"Brooke, I'm sorry. It's not that I didn't want to come. I have stuff going on. We just came back from a short trip, and I need to take care of—well you know, family stuff."

The blonde walked in and turned to her. "Family stuff? What, your uncle needs you to get more toilet paper for him or something?"

"That's not funny, Brooke."

"I think it is. Remember that time at the Gasparilla Parade in Tampa when he couldn't find a Port-A-Potty in time and had that accident, right there on Seventh Avenue? OMG it was the rage!"

Sierra didn't even crack a smile. "Yeah, I remember…"

"We talked about it for days at school!"

"Uh, I think you need to leave Brooke."

"Or what? You know, Sierra, everyone talks about you behind your back. 'She's so beautiful, but she's so weird'. I try and cover for you. I tell them 'She's not weird, it's her weird uncle. Ha…"

The raven-haired beauty held in her rage and forced a smile. "Brooke, you remember that night when Hurricane Sam hit and the two of us were on the beach? Do you remember why we were there? Because you kept making fun of my uncle? Of my life? Do you remember that night?"

As the blonde bombshell reminisced in her mind, the smile slowly faded. She remembered the look in Sierra's eyes; she remembered that for the first time in her life she feared for her life. And she remembered telling everyone what happened and no one believed her. It was truly one of the most humiliating events in her life. Luckily for her, only she and Sierra knew it, and Sierra wasn't the gossiping kind. She gazed back up at her school rival.

"Oh? I'm sorry, Sierra, didn't mean to offend," she told her.

"Brooke, honestly, I think you just need to leave. There's no apology from a person like you that could possibly sound real. You're a narcissist, and unless you're the center of attention you won't even understand the human condition." She pointed to the open door.

Brooke turned, stopped, then turned back. "Humph! Well, on another note, just got my hair done, and I wanted you to see it. I put it on mom's tab. She's going to flip when she sees it when they get back. Aren't I ravishing?" she strutted out the door.

"You're something." The door slammed shut after her, just as the Zephyrhills water delivery man was approaching the elevator, holding a full bottle. Not seeing her, he bumped her, then bounced back against the brick wall. Sierra opened the door and glanced out.

"You idiot," Brooke screamed at the man. "You trying to kill me or something? I can have your job for this!"

The jug slipped from his hand, landed hard on the floor

with just enough force for all the water to burst out of the lid that popped open and strategically wash Brooke down from head to toe, totally demolishing her hairdo. The water only mysteriously seemed to find the young teen as a target, not the wall, floor, elevator door, or even the man carrying it. The blonde was the focus, and it hit her with a vengeance.

Sierra giggled. Yep, you look ravishing.

Nelson walked out to her. "Uh, did I miss something?"

"No Uncle Nelson, life as usual."

"Well, I left word with my doctor's office. I have to see why I have this indigestion issue. It's really cramping my style."

"Cramping. Was that pun intended, Uncle Nelson?"

"Ha, good one. Nope, it wasn't. Well, I'm gonna watch the game. Rays versus the Yankees. That's always a good game. You in?"

"I'll make the popcorn." She smiled.

"I'll pour the drink!"

In minutes the two were on the couch, heavily into the game. But during a commercial, Nelson turned to her.

"Sierra, so uh… you dating anyone?"

"Dating? No!" she chuckled.

"Don't you think Joey is cute?"

"Joey?"

"Don't Joey me. I see how he looks at you."

"Oh really?" she turned to face him on the couch.

"And exactly how does Joey look at me Uncle Nelson?"

"Same way that diver kid at Old Indian Lake looked at you, like you were a Barbie doll that he wanted to play with."

"Barbie? OMG you're so old school."

"Old school? At least I have a Twitter account!"

She tossed a handful of popcorn at him, and they laughed. Then his laugh withdrew and he stared at her, then slowly turned away.

"Uncle Nelson, what's wrong?"

He reached for his drink. "Nothing."

"No, come on… what? That smile just faded off your face and you went off into the Twilight Zone somewhere."

He put his drink down. "Sierra, have you seen pictures of Tina when she was young?"

"Mom?"

He nodded. "You look so much like her. You have her wit, her innocence, her smile. She was such an awesome friend, she became like the sister I never had. I feel like she's here with me sometimes."

"Aww."

"Did you know that when your sister was born, your mom asked me to be her god-father?"

"No."

"Yeah, your dad told me that at first she hadn't liked me, but I guess I proved myself worthy. Your parents were just so perfect for each other. I kept telling Joe that he hit the lottery with her. Then…"

They both turned away as grief slowly set in on both their faces. It was a topic they both tried to avoid if at all possible.

"Then they were gone," she added.

Nelson choked on a forthcoming tear for a second, then smiled. "He and I used to fight over who was going to walk you down the aisle. Then we came to an agreement, I'd walk you from the door to half-way up the aisle and then you'd take his arm there and walk the rest of the way up."

"Geez you guys were already planning my wedding for me?"

"It's what dads do."

A soft smile crept over her face, though sadness followed. "You make a great dad, Uncle Nelson."

"Yeah, yeah – that's what all my daughters say." He chuckled.

His cell phone went off just as he was about to raise the volume on the TV. "Oh man, I'd better get this. It's the developers again." He left the couch with his phone in one hand and his drink in the other hand and entered the kitchen.

Sierra curled up with the soft pillow next her and looked out the huge glass sliding door to her right. The Gulf of Mexico was her back yard, and at any given moment they could see swimmers, surfers, jet-skis, or boats out there. The view was ordinary for her. Even at night the shoreline was usually buzzing with activity.

Nelson slid his phone in his pocket as he approached the couch. The sheepish look on his face let her know that something was up. He had a habit of tracing the wrinkles on his forehead with his finger when something was truly bothering him.

"Uh… trouble?"

"No, not really—but, uh…well, the people from the development company, you know back in Old Indian Lake? Well, that was them on the phone." He paused.

"Yeah?"

"They really want to meet up with me. They bumped the meeting to tonight if I can make it, and I can… uh, you want to stay…?"

"No, Uncle Nelson," she interrupted quickly. "I wanna go back. I'll be ready in a second."

"Are you sure, honey? Because back in the hospital room you didn't seem like you ever wanted to step foot back in Old Indian Lake. I really kinda think you should stay home. You can fill me in on the score here. They're freaking tied!" He pointed at the television.

"Uncle Nelson, just go to the car. I'll be right there."

She ran off to her room, and he sighed in despair. "Really, Sierra, I'd feel a lot better if…"

"Will you stop? I'll be fine!"

"This better not have anything to do with that boy!"

"Just get your stuff." She slammed her door. "I'll be right down!"

He placed his empty glass on the coffee table and drew lines on his forehead. "Here we go again."

CHAPTER ELEVEN

Once again Sierra found herself at the shore of the lake, this time with Wilbur and the two brothers by her side.

"Sierra honey, for Christ's sake. Nelson made me promise him I wouldn't let ya in the water. He's going to go to his meeting, then he'll be right back. Ain't gonna take but maybe forty, forty-five minutes. So hang tight at in my office and for all that is sacred, girl, please don't get in the water," the old man pleaded. His voice shook anxiously. "I swear this feels like I just went back in time. I was telling your mother the same dad-gum thing!"

"Mr. Kettleman, I promise. I just needed to see it again, that's all. Uncle Nelson gave me such a hard time; But I insisted that he leave me here instead of my sitting in his car while he had his meeting. Honestly, I just want to see it one more time."

"It is peaceful, a lot more quiet than normal—right, Tyler?" Chris asked his older brother.

"Yeah, kinda freaky quiet." He stepped closer to Sierra as she took in the breeze off the water. "I'm glad you came back, Sierra. I thought I was never going to see you again."

"How could I not come back? I live right on the beach, and it's nothing like this. The lake is so different. I feel a surge of energy here."

The stillness of the night, the cool breeze over the lake, and nothing but crickets and an occasional hoot of an owl serenading the panorama was peaceful indeed.

"Sierra, you're one with the water. You know that, right?" Tyler asked.

"That's what they say about us two," his brother chimed in. "Like me and Ty were children of the sea or something. The three of us are just… different."

"No, Chris, Sierra is really one with the water. Us two? We like the water, but she…" he hesitated, then placed his hand on her shoulder.

She turned to him. "I what..?" was her response.

"She…"

"Sierra…" The wind spoke her name in a soft whisper. It sent a quick chill up the spine of everyone there but her.

"Okay, we just need to all come back in my cabin," the jittery elder said to the three. "Come on, now. I'll make hot chocolate for everybody, even marshmallows. Now just follow me."

"It's true," Chris said. "The lake really does call out your name. I heard it this time."

"No you didn't, boy." Wilbur smacked him on the back of the head.

"Ow!"

"Now listen to what I said and come back in the cabin. We can play some gin rummy 'til Nelson gets back from his meeting. I even got the wi-fi thingy on. Y'all can play games on my TV set. Now come on, all three of ya's."

"Sierra…"

"Dag nabbit, now you stop it! You stop it, ya hear!?" The old man ran to the shoreline, pulled off his baseball cap, showing his stringy white hair that went every which way, and was waving it out at the lake. "Leave the poor girl alone! Just stop it. Ya done took her family. Leave the girl in peace!"

Sierra walked out next to him, placed her arm in his, closed her eyes, and raised her other arm out to the calm waters.

"Sierra, wha… what you doing girl? Boys!? Get over here and cart this young lady back to the cabin, right this instant. Do you hear me? Or I'll get your grandma on the phone so fast your britches'll burn!"

"Sierra…"

He bent down and picked up a water-logged piece of wood and with all his might threw it out at the water. "I said stop it, lake! Stop it!"

The wood flew out maybe ten feet in front of them and froze in the air inches before it hit the water. It just hovered over the water as if a thin layer of air prevented it from landing.

"Whoa! Tyler, see that!?" Chris pointed out. "Pull out your phone, hurry!"

Sierra opened her eyes, dropped her hand, and the piece of wood landed in the water. PLOINK!

"What the…?" Tyler said.

Then out, deep in the middle of the lake, the ripples started up again. They were slow and almost unseen, but once the small waves started to hit the shore it was hard not to notice.

"Oh no, no!" The nervousness in Wilbur's cracking voice was noticeable to the brothers and easily understood.

"What the..?" Chris blurted.

"Boys, get this girl outta here, I don't care where you take her, just get outta here, now!"

Tyler jumped into action and reached for her and just at that moment they noticed a huge wave rush to the shore at lightning speed. Before they could react, it was on them, but stopped right at the shore. A nine foot wall of water stood still, right in front of Sierra billowing with the threat of an impending crash.

The cabin keeper gasped in amazement. Tyler stood in front of Sierra to shield her. Chris was filming the whole thing on his phone, capturing the wave-like sounds that seemed to halt in mid-air.

They all gasped when all of a sudden an opening started inside the wall of water. A line formed right in the middle and split straight up and straight down. Tyler backed up, trying to force Sierra to back up. The menacing wall of water defied gravity right in front of them while the opening widened to give them a view inside.

"What in the Sam Hill?"

The wave was slowly opening up into what looked like a corridor to an underwater cave.

"Sierra, come...."

She seemed mesmerized and inched forward toward the voice. The two brothers held her back; Chris dropped his phone in the water in the process.

"Leave her alone!" Wilbur screamed at the water. "I said leave her alone!" He was slapping at the wave with his hat.

The screeching of tires was the next thing they heard behind them, and Nelson was opening his back door.

"Get her in here now!" he screamed.

The brothers had her in their arms and rushed to the car, but the wave motioned and changed into the shape of an angry fist and slammed down hard on the sand, causing all of them to lose footing. Sierra was knocked unconscious and slowly drifted into the wave.

"No!" Tyler got up, ran with all his might, and landed in the water just in time to grab her.

"Chris! Help! Come on!" The two brothers and Nelson fought wave splashes one after another, splashes that were forcing them away from the shore while trying to pull her closer. Sierra was being pounded by them. It was as if the very lake took life and was determined to drag her in.

"You're killing her!" Wilbur screamed at the lake, "Dad-gum it, you want this girl to die?"

The forcing waves then suddenly retreated after the old man's cry. The water subsided and slowly receded back into its body.

"Wilbur, I think it understood you!" Chris screamed.

Sierra gasped for air and coughed out a throat full of lake water. Then Nelson saw blood on her forehead.

"Get her in the car. We're going back to the clinic!" he ordered.

v v v v v

In no time, the humming nurse was once again tending to the teenager.

"You just don't want to stay away, do you, dumplin'?"

"Huh? What happened?" Sierra was still groggy. She'd taken a hard pounding on the shore.

"Don't worry, baby; we'll get you back up in no time." Marjeanette smiled. She walked out as Nelson and Tyler came in.

"Sierra, the next time I suggest that you stay home…" he scolded, pointing at her.

"I know, Uncle Nelson." She rubbed her head. The bandage was soft, but there was a slight pain there when she touched it.

Tyler came up on the other side of the bed. He couldn't seem to hide his excitement. "Sierra, are you okay?"

"I–I think so."

"Uh, can you answer me something?"

She nodded her head.

"How exactly did that happen? I mean, what is it that makes the lake come alive when you're near it? I've heard all kindsa rumors, there's been legends, folklore, all kindsa stuff, but—wow, man. I saw it with my own two eyes! I've gotta get inside your head. I really want to know how…."

"Young man," Nelson interrupted.

"Huh?"

"Shut up."

"Yes sir."

Nurse Marjeanette strolled in with a young doctor. The Native American physician almost startled her when she saw him.

"Hi Sierra, I'm Doctor Moon."

"Moon? As in like… the moon?"

"Yes, Moon. So I hear we had somewhat of a disturbance at the cabin retreat?"

"Disturbance? Man, Doc, you don't know the half of it! The water came alive! She's like some kinda magnet or something and…" Tyler started.

"Young man," Nelson interrupted again.

"Huh? Oh, I know, shut up. I'm shutting up, sir."

The young doctor studied Tyler's excitement with a raised eyebrow as he came to a halt right next to the hospital bed.

"Hmm, water came alive, huh?"

"Yeah Doc, it was awesome, it was like…" he turned to Nelson who was shooting him back the look of death. Tyler stopped talking and made a zipper motion to his lips.

"I've spent many a weekend at Wilbur Kettleman's retreat. My people had a strong bond with the lake and the area."

"Well she has a bond too, Doc! I'm serious, you should…." he turned to Nelson again, "Okay. Maybe I just need to leave the room!"

"So, child of the water, are you?" he smiled at his patient.

"Child of the water?" she asked. She cocked her head at him in a curious stare. He simply smiled back.

They stared into each other's eyes. He knew something, and she had to know what he knew, but she didn't want to ask with everyone present. He turned to Nelson.

"Mr. Vargas, you are free to take Sierra back home tonight if you wish. I'd like her to stay overnight for observation, but it won't exactly be necessary. She'll be back."

"What do you mean she'll be back?"

The physician got closer to her, touched the skin under her eye, and stretched her eyelids. He stared into her eye for what seemed more than comfortably long. "Mm-hmm," he said. Then he turned around to walk out.

"Mm-hmm what? Wait a minute man, you don't just Mm-hmm and walk out. I need an explanation for Mm-hmm!" Nelson protested.

"Your daughter," Dr. Moon said, "is a very special case. You wouldn't be able to keep her away from Old Indian Lake if you tried. She was born here, and she'll die here."

He walked out. That sent Nelson into a rage.

"Hey, wait a minute, what the hell is that supposed to mean?" he rushed to the door, but Nurse Marjeanette, in her calm, smiling approach, backed him away.

"Now, now Mr. Vargas. Dr. Moon doesn't always exactly mean what he says when he says it. The best thing to do is get this child home and make sure she gets lots of rest," she reassured.

"Good, then we're going home and she'll get rest, and

Doc, she won't be back," he screamed at the now closing door, "Did ya hear me, Moon? She won't be back!"

Tyler was walking back in with a half-eaten protein bar. Nelson stopped him with a quick poke to his chest.

"You! Get her belongings! Come on Sierra, we're going home."

"Home?" Tyler whined.

"Home."

CHAPTER TWELVE

Home. It was the quickest he'd ever returned to St. Pete. By the time he had everything taken out of the car, brought back in the condo, and all put in place, she was relaxing on the couch.

"Sierra honey, I have to run the car to the mechanic for a second. I'm late on my oil change, and my regular mechanic, Mike on Treasure Island Beach, passed away. I'm going to try this new shop over on MLK. One of the guys told me about them, and they're open late. Are you going to be okay? You comfortable?"

"Yes, Uncle Nelson, I'm fine."

"Remember what Nurse Marjeanette said: You just need to rest. So rest, okay?"

"Yes, sir." She rolled her eyes.

"Okay, be right back. Maybe we can go to Biff Burger's when I get back." He smiled.

She replied with an "OK" sign.

Holding the TV remote in his grip, he pressed a couple of buttons, then dropped it on the sofa. "Be right back."

He reached for the doorknob and stepped out. As the front door slammed after him, he stood outside in the hallway, paused, and looked back at the door, wondering if she'd stay or go somewhere.

What am I going to do with that girl? he wondered to himself.

Nelson definitely had a lot on his shoulders. After Sierra's father died, he was left with full ownership of the partnership, and he didn't skip a beat. Taking on the added responsibility of raising Sierra was something he wasn't actually prepared for but willingly did so. She had no one else. She was such a vulnerable child, and for months he often found her in bed crying and calling out for her parents. No consoling he tried could break her of it. As she grew older, he'd find her outside, staring at the shoreline. It was like she was drawn to it. He even caught her walking to the shoreline in her sleep, something that he always found peculiar. She'd never actually walk into the water; she would just stare at it from the shoreline. Sure, living on the beach was almost anyone's dream, but the teen had a different approach to beach life.

Nelson boarded the elevator as he reflected back on the time she was eleven and had told him that she felt she too, like her family would die in the water. He had asked her, "Why do you think that, sweetheart?"

"I don't know, Uncle Nelson. Something about water calls me. It soothes me, but it also scares me. And it's not like the scary feeling I get watching a scary movie or when I have to get a shot at the doctor's. It's a different kind of scary. Like something deep inside me just knows."

That, coming out of the mouth of an eleven-year-old, didn't make the new single dad feel any better, knowing that the water lay just a few feet away from their back door, even if it was three stories up.

Meanwhile, inside the condo, Sierra's eyes grew heavy. She lay back on the couch. Nelson had purposely left reruns of The Joy of Painting on DVD playing. He knew that Bob Ross, the famous painter of the 1980s show, who was known for his soothing, tranquil voice would put her to sleep. It was what he'd used when she was a little girl, and it never failed. And sure enough, she was soon nodding off on the huge couch she had all to herself. She thought of Tyler, his smile, his blue eyes, the way he had held her in his strong arms when she faced the terrifying wall back at the lake. She smiled and calmly fell asleep.

It couldn't have been more than a minute after she felt herself nod off that she heard the annoying quick, impatient sound of knocking on glass. The front door was made of wood, but the sliding door on the balcony was a huge window. Their condo was on the third floor, though, so could someone have climbed up to get her attention? She nudged her chin with her palm after that thought.

"Sierra?"

She opened her eyes. She knew she had heard the knocking and then faintly heard her name.

"Sierra?"

She pulled the comforter off and looked at the glass,. There was a shadow on the other side of the curtain.

"Who's there?"

Whoever the annoying visitor was, they were standing there constantly rapping on the glass to the point that it was starting to irritate her. She threw the comforter on the floor, got up, and almost fell back on the couch from a slight dizzy spell. The gauze bandage was still on her temple. She slowly peeled it off and dropped it on the couch.

"Who..? Wait, I'm coming," she called, "I swear, if it's Brooke, I'm going to push her over the balcony."

She walked over to the glass door, then pulled the chain to open the curtain, hoping it wasn't her pest of a schoolmate or another of the neighborhood friends vying for her attention. Not even Joey, and she kind of liked him. She quickly learned that it was none of the possible guests she might have expected, and glared wide-eyed at the sight before her. Her family was standing there on the other side of the glass. She followed each of them with her eyes, from her father to her mother to her baby sister, whose green eyes almost sparkled from the glare of the glass pane. Then her eyes started to fill with tears.

"Mom?"

Her mother's sad, worn expression slowly turned into a smile that only a caring mother could give. Tina placed her hand on the glass, and Sierra slowly followed, raising her hand to meet her mom's to the point of almost touching. Then she banged angrily on the glass door.

"Stop it! Stop it. You're not here! You're dead! You're all dead! Stop it! Why are you doing this to me?"

Frustrated and suddenly overcome with bitter tears, she backed away from the glass, but to her astonishment they walked in, right through the closed glass door, and approached her.

"No, stop it! You're in my mind. Get out of my mind!"

She crouched down angrily, slapping both sides of her head. But they circled her, Joe first, and held her in a soft, loving hug. Soon Tina and Breanna did the same, and the Russo family was once more together. Whether this was real or not, the young girl could not hold it together anymore, and she broke down.

"Daddy! Why are you doing this to me? Why are you all coming back in my mind? You don't exist. You can't… I saw you die. You went down and never came back up! They never even found your bodies! Running Deer made this all up to play with my head; you're all trying to make me crazy! Please! I love you, but please leave me alone! You're torturing me!"

"No, honey, we aren't torturing you. We have no intention of harming you. But Sierra, we need you. Running Deer needs you. Old Indian Lake needs you. Baby, you have to come back. Please come back."

"No! You're not here anymore, Daddy! Stop it!"

She closed her eyes and dropped her face to the floor in agonized tears. Joe saw her pain, and it wasn't something he wanted to continue to inflict on his firstborn.

"Please, Daddy, stop."

That caused him to step back, and he pulled Breanna away, but Tina bent down to her, brushed back her long, dark hair, and held Sierra's face up to hers. She kissed her daughter's moist, tear-soaked cheek, then caressed her face with her hand. Somewhere in the background, Sierra heard a rush of running water, like a faucet had been left on, but she knew she was home alone.

"Sierra honey, we don't meant to cause you any more pain than you have had to deal with all your life."

Sierra looked up at her. "Then why...?"

"Honey, you are a child of the water."

The puzzled look on her face told Tina what would come next.

"Child of the... that crazy doctor said that! What does that mean, Mom? You gave birth to me, what does that mean?" Sierra was bewildered, in tears, and sobbing out loud enough that the neighbors might possibly hear.

"Honey, ask Tyler to take you to the spring. Just ask him. Do this for me, sweetheart, and then you'll understand." Her mother smiled, stroking back Sierra's hair. "Okay?"

"What? What spring?"

"Just ask him. He'll know. Sierra baby, I love you."

That was the last straw. Sierra was now fully on the floor, face down, punching the carpet in anguish.

"Mom if you loved me you'd stop tormenting me so much! Leave me alone! Why don't you all just leave me alone!?"

"We can't."

"You have to! You're not real. You're not real!" She kept

repeating it to herself and holding her hands to her ears to keep their voices out. Her mother's voice faded away, yet the sound of rushing water that she had heard before never subsided, and to her surprise, it was getting louder.

If Sierra Russo ever had been at the point of losing it, this was the moment. Between the anger, the sorrow, and the hurt of her family gone all these years, then seeing them materialize in front of her, it was truly too much for her heart to bear, and she began a wave of uncontrollable deep and bitter heartfelt sobs.

"Sierra? Sierra, you need to stop this."

She felt a strong arm on her shoulder, and it started to shake her.

"Sierra!?"

"Stop it!" She swung her arm out in rage and connected.

"Oh!"

Sierra opened her eyes. She was back in bed at the clinic and sat up in a quick fit. Tyler was flying back away from the force of her punch and fell over the chair in the room and crashed onto the wet floor. In her sleep she had punched him across the jaw. There was water all over the floor, and the faucet was on, its contents spewing out of the hose attached to it in full force. But instead of following the flow of gravity, the water was floating in the air and moving about like a snake all throughout the room. Nurse Marjeanette was rushing into the room to see what the commotion was about, only to stumble into the horror when she witnessed Dr. Moon's predicament.

The young doctor, who had chosen to revisit the new patient at Old Indian Lake Clinic, was standing at Sierra's bedside. He, like Tyler, had been trying to revive her, but the water had circled his throat like a rope, and he was calling out his patient's name in panic.

"Sierra?!"

Tyler jumped back up, and grabbed her by the shoulders, and forced her back down on the pillow.

"Sierra, stop this, right now! Stop it!"

She flew out of her trance just in time, because the liquid rope was squeezing tighter on the physician's neck.

"T… Tyler?" she gasped.

Her eyes flew open, and the handsome diver was right in her face. She turned around to witness her handiwork. The water was bouncing around the room as if it were possessed with a life of its own somehow.

"Sierra, you're going to hurt the doc. Stop it! He's not the bad guy."

She spun around and looked at the young doctor gasping for breath, then at the elderly nurse, and the fear in Marjeanette's eyes made Sierra cringe.

"Oh my God! Stop!" Sierra screamed.

She stretched out her arm and opened her palm wide. At that instant, all the water that was floating around the room dropped to the floor in a loud splash. Doctor Moon, the thin, wiry twenty-something resident physician, fell to the floor in a faint. Sierra reached out and grabbed Marjeanette in a strong grip and brought her closer to the bed, holding her in a strong hug, then started crying, shaking uncontrollably.

"I'm sorry, I'm so sorry Nurse Marjeanette! I'm sorry!"

Tyler finally fell back away against the wall with a huge

sigh of relief, rubbing his jaw. Then he bent down to help Dr. Moon to his feet.

"It's okay, baby. You're going to be okay. Yes indeed. You had us worried there for a while, though. You were talking to your parents in your sleep. Now that business with the water, that was just…I don't know."

"Fate." The doctor coughed, trying to stand. "Eyaha hocteh cheh." He pointed at her. "Eyaha hocteh cheh!" He stumbled out of the room, holding his neck.

"What does that mean? Freaky," Tyler said.

"Freaky, that's what I was thinking." The nurse smiled at Tyler before turning to Sierra. "Baby, are you okay?" Marjeanette held her in a loving hug, and Sierra kissed her cheek.

"He didn't say freaky. He called me a…." Then she turned to Tyler. "Well, never mind."

"Sierra, are you going to be okay?"

"Tyler, I…I'm sorry, I… I can't…."

"You can't control it, right?" Tyler smiled.

"Control it, yes… you know about this, this thing I have?"

"Yeah, uh, Wilbur told me about it. You have some kinda supernatural power over water; he believes that the old Indian gave you this power when you were born. He used to babble about it all the time. I always thought he was a crazy old man—all of us did. But I just saw it with my own two eyes, again. That was… amazing, Sierra. Freaky but amazing."

"Tyler, you say Wilbur told you about an old Indian?" Marjeanette asked. "What are you two kids talking about?"

Sierra looked past her at the wall, where a scene with Running Deer and a wolf by his side was the main image of a wall calendar. She pointed at it.

"Him. That's him! That's Running Deer. And," she paused, "a wolf. That's what Dr. Moon called me: a wolf girl."

"Wolf girl? Sounded like Greek to me! How do you know what he said?" Tyler asked. He held her hand.

"I don't know."

Marjeanette faced the huge calendar, which was familiar to her; the calendar was a copy of one that was in almost every business in Old Indian Lake, Florida, and was distributed by the development company that was building in town. They had more of this calendar than they knew what to do with.

"Uh, honey, you realize, if you're talking about this man right here, then he's been dead for more than 180 years, right?" The nurse smiled. She glanced out the door. Dr. Moon was talking to another doctor and pointing at Sierra. Tyler was on the other side of the bed, softly massaging her back.

"Dead? Well, yes, but he… he…." she blinked in confusion, then faced Tyler, who smiled back at her.

"Sierra, just lie back and relax," he said.

"I don't understand, Tyler. What's going on?" she asked.

He shrugged his shoulders and covered both her hands with his.

"I mean, how did I get here? I went home, didn't I? With Uncle Nelson? Didn't we leave?"

"No, you've been here all the time," he said. "Your uncle's been in a meeting with those developers in the waiting room.

And from the looks of it, I think you guys are going to be living on easy street soon."

"How long have I been here?"

"Just only a few hours, baby." Marjeanette smiled.

Just then Nelson walked in with a cup of coffee and almost slipped on the still-slick floor.

"Hey, what happened in here?"

"Just a little water play." The giggling nurse smiled. "Nothing to worry about. We'll get someone in here to mop it right up. Yes indeedy."

"Honey, are you okay?" He handed his cup to Tyler after pulling the young man's grip from Sierra's shoulder. "Geez." He grimaced.

"Yes Uncle Nelson, I'm fine. Aren't I, Nurse Marjeanette?"

"I wouldn't think so, but if it means you want to leave…". The nurse sighed. "… then you're good as peaches." She was squeezing water from the wash towel that she'd used to sop up the drenched countertop.

"So, we can leave?"

Marjeanette called for Dr. Moon, who refused to step in the room. He motioned for her to go. The nurse cupped Sierra's chin in her caring hand. "Yes, honey, you sure are, yes indeed, time for you to get up and go home."

"Home, Sierra, are you ready to go home?" Nelson asked. He took his cup out of Tyler's grip and quickly gulped down the entire drink.

She and Tyler shared a stare into each other's eyes that seemed too long for Nelson. He snapped his fingers. "Hello?" He raised his eyebrow, awaiting her answer. "Sierra?" He drew a line on his forehead with his finger.

"Uh, no. I think I want to stay here for a little bit. Is that okay, Uncle Nelson?"

"Well sure, honey, but…uh…I have some work to do downtown. The developers want me to see their plans and see how I can help secure their servers after the initial scope of work. Nothing out of the ordinary for me—a few algorithms to create and I can…" He looked around at the blank faces. "Uh, work talk, sorry… anyway after that I'll have to get back to St. Pete, then come back tomorrow."

"She can stay with Wilbur at the lake. Old Wilbur won't mind." Tyler smiled. "If that's okay with you? He'll give her a cabin of her own and she can…."

"No." Nelson turned to him. "I don't want you at that lake, Sierra. I feel better with you coming home with me."

"Honey, if you need a place to stay, I have an extra room in my house." The nurse smiled. "Besides, they keep me working here so much, and someone has to feed my cat. You like cats?"

Nelson frowned at the woman, then turned to Sierra. "I, uh…."

"I will take care of your baby, Mr. Vargas."

He hesitated.

"I'll be fine, Uncle Nelson. I want to look up some, stuff. There's a reason I'm here. I need to know. Go do your business. After all, Joseph-Nelson never lets a customer down." She smiled. "Then tomorrow I'll go back home with you."

Nelson looked at her; then his eyes moved over to Tyler, and he wondered if what she wanted to look up was the young rugged diver reaching to hold her hand again.

"Uh, then again, maybe I should stay here. Business can wait."

"No, she'll be fine here. I'll watch over your baby girl. She's a native child; she needs to be home for a while," Marjeanette said.

Nelson turned to the nurse.

"I'll be fine, Uncle Nelson, really. I won't go to the lake."

"I'll be her bodyguard, Mr. Nelson," Tyler offered, showing off his biceps.

That was part of what he was afraid of. "Okay, against my better judgment, young man, I'm going to trust you and Marjeanette here. This is my baby. She's my life. But I'll be back tomorrow. Marjeanette, how much trouble can they get into?"

"I know Tyler, and I know his grandmamma. Your baby is in good hands, Mr. Vargas."

Nelson hugged the nurse, then leaned over and kissed Sierra.

"I'll be fine. I have a backpack in the trunk with all my stuff."

"Oh, I see." He smirked.

She got up off the bed, and he took her hand. "Thank you, Nurse Marjeanette," she said.

"Any time, baby."

Tyler followed them out the door, and they met at Nelson's car outside. Dr. Moon, standing at the station, eyed her all the way until she left the lobby area. Nelson opened the trunk and pulled out the backpack that she had lightly packed for their trip back home; it was almost like she knew she was going to stay.

"Young man, your car somewhere near?"

"Uh, I have a bike sir, that Harley over there?"

Sierra took the bag and strapped it on.

"Motorcycle? Wait a min—"

"Uncle Nelson, I'll be fine."

Nurse Marjeanette came out, handed Sierra a key and a hospital business card with her handwriting on the back.

"Young man, you know where Chestnut Street is? The number is 1725. My cat's name is Sebastian. He'll act shy and all at first, but if you sit on the floor and talk to him, he'll just purr in your lap. Yes indeedy. He gets talkative late in the night though. Give him a treat and he'll just follow you all over the house."

"Thank you Nurse Marjeanette." Sierra smiled.

"And you're going to drop her off, then go home to Grandma's. Right, young man?" Nelson pointed at him.

"Yes sir, I promise."

Sierra bounced glances off the two, but a quick flashback of her mother from the dream came front and center. She blinked twice.

"Leave me alone!"

"We can't."

No one else heard the internal struggle of the fifteen-year-old. She shook her head to ward Tina off.

"Don't worry, Mr. Vargas—Nelson—Uncle—sir. I'll be her protector." Tyler smiled.

Nelson looked nervous but then felt the stomach discomfort happen again.

"Oh boy…."

"Bathroom?" Sierra smiled.

He nodded and ran back into the clinic building.

"You two stay out of trouble, or that poor man will have a coronary." The nurse chuckled. She followed him back to the door.

"Nurse Marjeanette, do you have anything that could help Uncle Nelson with his indigestion issue? It's been bothering him ever since I can remember."

"Hmm, I'll just have to take a look into that," she called as she strode back into the building. The two new friends walked over to the Harley.

"Aren't you kinda young for a bike like this, Tyler? It looks like it could be a classic or something."

"It is. It was my grandfather's, then my dad's. He says it's mine on my birthday when I turn eighteen. She's beautiful, isn't she? Man, when these came out my granddad begged his mom to let him get it. A 1971 FX 1200 Super Glide. This baby has an air-cooled, four stroke, V-Twin. She glides like the wind. I modded the..."

The blank, glassy stare she shot back at him was something he was accustomed to.

"Oh...not into motorcycles, huh?"

"Well, they look nice on the road; but Uncle Nelson says they're too dangerous."

"That, my dear," and he smiled, climbing on, "depends on who's driving."

He started the bike, and she put her helmet on and held him around the waist. He was waiting for that. It brought a bright smile to his face.

"When's your birthday?"

"October 30th. Halloween's always a fun time at my

house, I get to celebrate two holidays, ha. So, 1725 Chestnut Street, madam?"

"1725 it is, but I'm kinda in the mood for ice cream first." She smiled.

"Ice cream, mmm, I know just the place."

They sped down the two-lane highway.

CHAPTER THIRTEEN

Hours later, Nelson was on the highway, headed back home alone. The phone went off just as he was popping a CD in the stereo. He tapped the hands-free button on his steering wheel, dropping the CD on the floor in the process. "Yello, it's Nelson."

"Nelson?"

"Wilbur, my man. You finally got around to listening to my message to call me back?"

"Yep, sorry there, buddy. I was trying to clean up around here, Marty just replaced my busted toilet and plumbing. It was a mess. You remember Marty, right? From over on 14th Avenue? His wife passed away last year. Sad story…."

"Yeah, I remember Marty." He wanted to cut him off before he got started.

"Well then, them dad-gum developers called wantin' to talk to me again. I keep telling them I don't want nothing to do with their plans to make changes in Old Indian Lake. Nelson if I knew they were so much trouble I woulda never recommended you to them, dang-blast it!"

"Wilbur, come on, man. Change is good. They have an awesome vision; I saw the plans they have for the cabin area. You need to reconsider, but look, that's not why I called. Sierra's there. She's staying in town. Nurse Marjeanette is letting her stay at her place…uh, do you know Marjeanette?"

"Do I Know Margie? Are you kiddin'? Me and Marj go way back. We met in 1986 at the crawfish festival—yep, April 1986—man, I never got so full on crawfish in my life, 'cept that time at Mardi Gras back in '75. Boy oh boy, they had 'em grilled, buttered, fried, baked, steamed, boiled—you ever had 'em boiled? Nelson, you don't know what you're missing. That reminds me of the time…."

"Okay, okay, Wilbur. Look, I just need you to go check on her, okay? That Tyler kid gives me the creeps, and…."

"Tyler? Tyler Phillips? The diver? Nelson, Tyler's a good kid. You ain't got nothin' to worry about with Tyler."

"Nothing to worry about? Look he's a boy, she's a girl. Don't you remember how you were at eighteen?"

There was silence for a few seconds.

"Wilbur?"

"Heh, yeah… I was just reminiscing, now that cha

mention it. Man I wonder what ever happened to Suzette? Heard she moved down to the Keys with some French guitar player named Paul… something. Man, that girl owned my heart, Nelson. She was Raquel Welch, Marilyn Monroe, and Ann-Margret all rolled up into one beautiful, irresistible thang…well, with a little Elizabeth Taylor thrown in for good measure! Whoo doggy! Uh, you know who Ann-Margret is, right?"

"Geez, Wilbur, just do me a favor and check, will ya? I'm already feeling like I made a mistake. Man I shouldn't have left her, maybe I need to turn around."

"Why'd ya leave, anyways?"

"I have to get my laptop, hard drives, and scopes. I have a major presentation with the developers, and I wasn't as prepared as I planned, what with everything going on with Sierra. I'll be back in the morning, so I'm serious, man, I need you to…."

"Nelson, I'll make sure the girl is all right!" he interrupted. "Why didn't you just have her stay here in one of the cabins?"

"Are you kidding? I don't want her anywhere near that lake— understand me, Wilbur? That's the rule: Keep her away from the lake. Promise me, man. I mean it!"

"Tarnation, boy. Keep your shirt on. I know where Marjeanette lives. I'll give her a call in a minute—satisfied? Hell, don't cha trust the girl?"

"She's not the one I don't trust, Wilbur!"

The old man smacked his teeth on the phone.

"Okay, I'll check for ya."

"Thanks."

v v v v v v v v

Back on the front porch at 1725 Chestnut Street, Tyler and Sierra were seated on the old wooden swing that hung on rusted chains. The cool breeze felt good on this humid Florida night. Tyler's hand was in hers, and they were staring into each other's eyes.

"Wow, Sierra, that's really a sad story. I mean, you saw your whole family disappear into the lake. I can't even imagine the anguish you lived through."

"Yeah...I've had to live with it all my life—well, most of it, anyway."

"Man I don't know what I'd do if I lost Mom, Dad, my brother, or even my grandma."

"I wouldn't wish it on anyone, Tyler."

"So your uncle's been your whole family, then, since your grandmother died soon after."

"Yeah, I love Uncle Nelson, just sometimes…."

"Hey, the old man cares about you. I can see that a mile away. He didn't even want to trust me, and everyone trusts me."

"Well, he doesn't know you." She rested her head against his chest, and he caressed the back of her head, brushing back her long hair in his hand.

The screen door opened, and Marjeanette walked out, holding fresh-baked cookies in her hand while speaking on the phone. "Yes Wilbur, she's fine. Tyler is just about to leave. No, Vikki offered to cover my shift tonight so I could come home early. Just finished a fresh batch of oatmeal raisin cookies. Want to come by tomorrow at the clinic and pick

130

some up?"

The cat was curled up in Sierra's lap.

"Yes Wilbur, Tyler is leaving any minute. Tell that Nelson friend of yours to calm down already."

"I guess that's my cue." Tyler smiled.

"Can you come pick me up tomorrow?"

"I'll be here. Bye, Nurse Marjeanette." He grabbed a handful of cookies, kissed Marjeanette on the cheek, and then did the same to Sierra.

"Bye Sebastian."

The cat didn't even acknowledge him.

In seconds he was on his bike and peeling away down the lone road.

"Ready for bed, Sierra? I have your room all set up."

"Okay."

As she stood, the cat hopped on the wooden bannister and started hissing out into the dark.

"Sebastian?" his owner called.

HSSSSSS

"Sebastian, what's wrong?" Sierra patted his back. The cat never took his sights off the bushes across the street.

"Is someone out there?" Marjeanette called. She reached over and took the broom in her hand. Sierra stood and glared out into the bushes. She saw a pair of red eyes staring back from far out.

"What… what's that?" she pointed.

Marjeanette didn't see them, but Sebastian did. Before either of them could act, the huge black cat hopped off the porch and dashed across the street, emitting a howl that his owner had never heard before.

"Awoooooooooo!" replied another howl in the brush across the street.

"Sebastian!" Sierra grabbed the broomstick and leapt off the porch, chasing the cat.

"Oh dear," Marjeanette sighed. "Sierra honey, don't go out there!"

Sierra stopped at the edge of the dark street, stared in, squinting hard to focus. The annoying buzz of mosquitoes whizzing by her face distracted for just a few seconds as she swatted them away. Suddenly the sound of two animals at a stand-off almost made her cringe.

"Sebastian! Come!" she called.

She looked around; whatever had caught the protective pet's attention was surely trying to keep its own. The eerie howls filled the air and quickly worried Sierra.

"Sebastian!"

Seconds after she screamed his name, the feline quickly dashed by her and ran back to the house. Sierra stepped into the high grass. "Who's there?"

"Sierra honey, please come back to the house. Your uncle will kill me if something were to happen to you," the elder nurse called from her porch. "Please, Sierra."

There was movement out in front of her. She thought she heard a growl, and she held the stick up above her head in her best baseball batter pose. "I'm not afraid of you, come out! Why are you hiding?"

"Sierra…"

It was faint, but she heard her name come out of the tall grass, followed by the distinct odor of musk. It was clearly the smell of a wild animal. "Geez." She waved the air around her face.

It was close enough for her to smell, but she couldn't see it. But for some reason she wasn't afraid. Then that scent was quickly covered by a hint of shoreline. To someone connected to water, it's a pleasing aroma, be it salt or fresh water. Sure, the echo of crickets and the disturbing noise of insects circled her too, but the glistening hum of water lapping on the shore was almost a constant soundtrack to her—whether she was near water or not. It quickly drowned out the musky smell that had surrounded her.

"Sierra."

Hearing her name in the wind was starting to become a normal thing in this town. It didn't catch her by surprise like the first time she heard it at the lake, but she still stepped back to try to pinpoint its origin. Just at that moment, the red eyes approached her. Finally she saw the form of a dog— or a large wolf—slowly approaching. And right behind it….

"Running Deer!"

He stopped right in front of her, motioning for her to lower the stick. She did.

"Why are you following…?"

"You remained for a reason," he softly interrupted, "to quench your curiosity, to find out why your heart yearns to return here. Your blood will always remain here; your soul craves to understand the circumstances of your origins."

She stood still, almost as if his soothing words were putting her in a trance.

"My child, you are searching for answers. I have your answers. They are within reach. Come, follow me." He stretched out his hand.

She dropped the broomstick on the ground and stared at him, then reached out her hand, stared at the wolf, then back up at him, then yanked her hand back. "No."

"Chackshosti, a-la-kus-cheh," he uttered.

"No, I will not follow you, and stop calling me 'daughter'!"

"Sierra, who are you talking to?" the voice of Marjeanette was coming up behind her.

"Wee-ki-vah." He patted his wolf, and they both walked back into the woods.

She watched them walk back through the high grass, and she stared until they were out of range. Then she repeated what he had last said. "Spring of water…."

Marjeanette had finally made it across and managed to navigate through the tall, thick, unkempt grass to meet her. "Honey, please come back in the house. Lots of wild animals out there in the woods, you know? You never know if there's a Florida panther, a coyote, wolf…."

"Yes, ma'am."

"Wolf." The word replayed in her mind for a few seconds.

They crossed the street as the creepy howl of the wolf once again filled the air. They both turned back. It was distant, but still creepy enough for the nurse to take Sierra by the arm and rush her back to the porch.

"Marjeanette, do you know where the spring is?"

"The spring? Yes honey, why?"

"I think… I kinda think I need to see it. Can you take me there tomorrow?"

Marjeanette placed her hand on Sierra's back.

134

"Sweetheart, tomorrow's another day. Let's get back in the house. You need your rest. Now, who were you talking to out there?"

"Uh…" she thought about it, let it mull in her mind a few seconds. Mentioning a legend of the town who had been dead for over 180 years probably wouldn't come out right, no matter how she said it. "No one, Miss Marjeanette." She smiled. "Just the wind. It kinda creeps me out."

The old wooden screen door slapped shut behind them.

CHAPTER FOURTEEN

Sleep was always an issue for Sierra. Some nights she'd sleep peacefully through the night, but then other nights she was up several times, tossing and turning from a horrid nightmare involving her family or a vague representation of Running Deer. He could be a myriad of animals in her night visions: an owl, a hawk, a snake… a wolf. Countless nights she'd wake up in a screaming sweat, panting, crying, and Nelson would rush into her room to calm her. But last night's sleep was one of the rare peaceful slumbers she hadn't remembered experiencing in a long time.

By the time she had woken up, Marjeanette was already gone to work, and she lazily sat up on the queen-sized canopy bed. The bright Florida sun rays sprinkling in through her sheer curtain let her know it was time to get up, but the heaviness of the purring cat lying right next to her made her want to stay in bed and purr right beside him. "Sebastian, why can't I just stay in bed and be lazy like you? You have the best life. I bet you don't have dreams with talking owls."

She stroked his back, and he began a long drawn-out stretch at the mere touch of her hand. After a long yawn, she glared out the window at the bushes across the street. They didn't seem as menacing as they had last night, just high grass that needed serious lawn care and a forest right behind it that seemed to stretch forever. She reached for her phone.

"Ten-fifteen—wow, I really had a good sleep. I never wake up this late. Hmm, two missed texts."

She scrolled through them. The first one—as she might have guessed—was from Uncle Nelson: "Honey, I'm taking care of business here at home, then headed back to Old Indian Lake later than I thought. Call me when you get up. Marjeanette says you were sleeping like a baby, and I didn't want her to wake you up, Love, Unk. And stay away from that boy!"

The next text helped fully wake her up. "Sierra, coming to pick you up at 10:30, Tyler… TTYL."

"OMG!"

The fifteen-year-old hopped out of bed.

By the time she was ready, the familiar roar of Tyler's bike filled the entire street, let alone Marjeanette's small house. She was holding Sebastian in her arms as she approached the front door. Tyler was already on his second step up the three wooden stairs. Marjeanette's house was typical for Old Indian Lake: wood frame, wooden porch, wood screen door, and ready for another paint job to cover the faded white that was currently adorning its exterior, and maybe ready for a new roof in another year or two. The small two-bedroom house lay almost outside the city limits. Nature was her closest neighbor. Travelers coming in from the north getting off the highway would pass the "Welcome to Old Indian Lake, Florida" sign, then pass her house on the small dirt road coming into town.

Tyler stepped toward the screen door; the one loose board gave him away as it squeaked under his weight. She put Sebastian down on the couch, strapped her Coach cross-body purse over her shoulder then exited the house toward him.

"Well, good morning, beautiful." He smiled.

"I bet you say that to all the girls."

"Nah, just raven-haired natural glamor girls who were born here, then raised in St. Pete." He smirked. "Happens more than you know."

"And he's a comedian." She poked him on the chest.

"Ready to go?"

"Where?" she asked.

"Anywhere you want. It's your day. I'm here to serve,

m'lady." He bowed.

Sebastian meowed at the screen door.

"See?" She smiled at him. "Even Sebastian thought that was lame."

"Okay, that hurt." He stepped closer to her, touched her arm.

"You know, Tyler, Uncle Nelson says I need to stay away from you."

"Yeah, he doesn't like me for some reason."

"I think it's just because you're a boy, and I'm a girl."

He got closer to her. "Yeah, a beautiful, mysterious creature of a girl," He drew a line down her arm with his finger, "And it's that mystery part that makes you so attractive."

"Oh, I see." She stared into his eyes.

He got closer to her, but she stopped him with a light press against his chest. "Tyler, do you know where the spring is?"

"The spring? Well, uh, yeah, but what does that have to do with…."

"I need to go there."

"Why? Like now?"

"Yes, like now."

"Why?"

She took his hand in hers, kissed it. "I don't know. I was just told to ask you to take me there. Will you take me there?"

"Uh, okay, but who told you to ask me? Nurse Marjeanette?"

"No, come on." She yanked him toward his Harley.

They approached the bike and got on. She held him tight as he revved the engine.

"So, who told you to ask me?"

"Nobody, just my mom."

"Your mo—uh, ok, I'm not even going to ask."

"No, seriously."

"Yeah, okay."

The bike sped off down the main street.

CHAPTER FIFTEEN

The beautiful tropical scenery of the small town of Old Indian Lake, Florida was breathtaking—the kind one would see in a magazine about southern living or retirement ads. Sure, there were oak trees all over, and they were full of Spanish moss—something the Native Americans called "tree hair"—but there were also palm trees that lined the roads, scrub palmetto plants, swamp fern, orange trees, and grapefruit trees. The tropical climate of the third largest state of the Union is one of its highest selling points and brings people from all over to visit Florida. From the history of St

Augustine, the theme parks of Orlando, the beach coasts of Tampa Bay to the hustle and bustle entertainment of the metropolis of Miami Beach, there is always something to do in the Sunshine State. But the town of Old Indian Lake remains almost untouched because its tourists consist mostly of business convention attendees, who come here, do business, fish, then leave.

As the Harley cruised up the winding road next to the lake, Sierra took in all the sights. She grew up as a visitor to Old Indian Lake, although she was born here, but she'd never realized how beautiful this little town was. She held on as Tyler turned down the lone dirt road and sped through as leaves spit back from the tires' traction. They passed one of the few billboards in that region, a refurbished 20-foot tall sign advertising the new Old Indian Lake Visitor Complex currently in the planning stages and set for spring of the next year. She glanced around. She'd never been on a motorcycle before, and the speed was breathtaking. Then she turned to the right and stared at the calm body of water called Old Indian Lake. It was a huge oblong boomerang shape, which some said looked almost like the shape of Florida, and Wilbur's cabin retreat was at the bottom tail end. The place they were headed was at the top left of the boomerang, where the actual natural spring came out of a rock formation that the native Seminoles called E-fah E-ca.

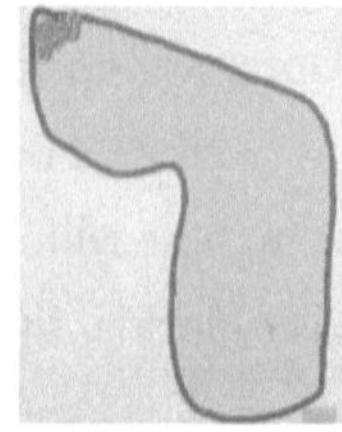

"Where is this place?" she called out.

"Almost there." he replied.

The motorcycle came to a slow halt and coasted to a clearing in the woods. He turned off the bike and pulled the kickstand   out with a swift stomp of his boot heel. She crept off the Harley and glanced around in a slow, awe-filled stare, taking in a whiff of fresh air. The area looked pure and untouched; it was awe-inspiring to her. He stepped away from the bike and climbed up to the rock formation, then pointed out into the vast lake that was just feet below him and spread his arms out wide.

"You like it? When the native Seminoles discovered this formation, they believed that spirits existed here from the ages…"

"E-fah E-ca." Sierra said in a whisper.

Tyler cocked his head and looked at her in a puzzled glare. There was a bronze plaque, and he was actually reading off of it, and she said the next words that were etched there, but he knew she couldn't see the plaque from where she stood. "Yeah," he said raising his eyebrow, "that's what they named it."

"It means Head of Dog, because the big rock you're standing on looks like a dog's head," she whispered to herself.

She turned to him, and he was staring at her, confused. "How do you know that?"

"I…I don't know."

Sierra looked around; the scene in front of her seemed straight from a movie where the camera was introducing the splendor of a paradise-like location, complete with a rock formation in the middle of the woods with crystal clear water spouting from the crevice and cascading down into a waterfall stream into a clear pool. Movie producers kill for a setting like this. The trees and shrubbery surrounding it reminded her of the Bob Ross paintings she was used to watching on the TV screen. "This is—wow, Tyler, this is beautiful, but…."

Tyler put his keys in his pocket and climbed back down to her. "But what?"

The cool breeze raced over the calm pool and rushed up to her. Her hair flew past her neck and back into Tyler's face and brushed up her short dress. It flapped in the wind in a manner reminiscent of the famous Marilyn Monroe scene from the movie Seven Year Itch. He walked around up to face her and took her hand. She looked around, bouncing her innocent eyes on the scene around her, then on Tyler.

"But…I've been here before. I've never seen this place before in my life, but I've been here. Tyler, this is one of the weirdest feelings I've ever had."

He smiled, held both her hands in his. "They call that a 'déjà vu moment,' Sierra. That's what you're experiencing. Sometimes people think…."

"No, Tyler, I'm serious. I've been here before. I just don't remember when, or…how."

"You're home, Sierra. This is home to you." He smiled, displaying perfect teeth.

"Huh?"

"I mean come on, face it, you were born here. Do you know how many people move away, then come back? You aren't the only one. There's something about Old Indian Lake that keeps its people home. Maybe when you were little your dad brought you up here to the view off the dog head and you don't remember. Think about it. That's possible, isn't it?"

She nodded in agreement because it sounded possible, but she didn't really agree that was it.

"I'm taking an online Marine Biologist semester at Miami U because I didn't want to leave," he continued. "When I graduate, I'm going to open the first mini aquarium here. It'll bring tourists like wild because there's something about the fish here."

"Well, that's true. Old Indian Lake's fish are definitely different, but…."

"And look at you, Sierra. You've had to deal with the tragedy of your family, then you moved away to live with your Uncle Nelson, but you were born here, and deep down inside you, somewhere—your heart, your body, your soul knows it—his is home. You had to come back, didn't you? Something inside you made you come back, right?"

She stared at him as he said it. She knew it was true, and she couldn't explain it.

"Yes, all my life I've felt the pull inside to come back. But Uncle Nelson just wouldn't have it. I don't know why. I have haunting dreams, and they are all connected to Old Indian Lake."

"Well, there you go. This is your destiny, Sierra, and you belong here. Stop fighting it. Personally, I love your being here. You're so unlike anyone I have ever met. You're special."

"Special, huh? Is that a compliment?"

"That's definitely a compliment."

He stared into her eyes. She knew what was coming next, but she didn't want to let it happen, though a part of her did. Tyler was so dreamy and so nice to her, and he always managed to say the right thing. He moved a lock of her hair away from her covered eyes.

"Sierra, I believe in fate, and I believe you're meant to be here. I'm just glad that somehow I have become involved in your journey. I mean that."

She stared into his blue eyes, then closed hers to eventually turn and gaze out at the calm, clear water below them.

"Tyler, you always say the right things. It's just so confusing."

"What's confusing?"

"Well, this. Standing here like this with you. I know what I'm feeling inside, but…."

"But?"

"I see Uncle Nelson's face and him rubbing his forehead saying, 'Stay away from that boy!'"

"You always listen to what he says, don't you?"

"Yes. He's the best thing that's ever happened to me. He's never failed me."

"I will never fail you either Sierra, I promise."

"I know, I believe you Tyler, but…."

"But what, Sierra?" he got closer.

Deep inside she knew she had to change the subject. She was here on a mission, and she wasn't going to let feelings get in the way, as badly as she wanted to right now. "But, this spring…what exactly is it?"

"Well," Tyler pulled away. He got the hint, so he sat on the rock overlooking the vast lake of fresh water and began, "As legend has it, there was an old Indian whose name was

Running Deer. When the white man decided he wanted to take this land by force, take it away from the tribe that had dwelled here for generations, Running Deer was determined to do something about it, because he knew it was totally wrong of them. Rumor had spread among his people that their lands were quickly being gobbled up by settlers, and this new breed of people who called themselves Americans. They and their ancestors all came from Europe and came here to their land at first to share, but later to conquer and invade. Even the military was in on the takeover.

"An army regiment came to this region and thought they'd found Ponce DeLeon's fountain of youth when one of the men jumped in to wash himself and walked out with his bullet wounds healed and war scars completely wiped off his face. That's the legend anyway. They formed a small band of rebels, determined to make this their land, but the Indians fought back."

"They lost the battle," she said, almost as if in a trance. "They were mercilessly slaughtered like animals."

"Yeah. They were." He raised one eyebrow again because she always seemed to finish his sentences when it came to Old Indian Lake history. "And, uh, well anyway, Running Deer swore he would never leave his land, the land of his fathers and of the Great Spirit."

"And he dwells here still today fighting to protect the home of his ancestors and family. Tyler, he's calling me. He's been haunting me all of my life. I've been here before, I just…I just I don't remember how or when," She shook her head. "It actually hurts my head just thinking about it."

"Running Deer was killed here. It was his last stand."

"I—I feel that I know that. Oh Tyler, what's wrong with me?"

He got closer to her, held her in a soft hug.

"Sierra, I was born and raised here. The older folk talk about people being in tune with the spirits, that they recapture scenes and emotions from the past, especially when they are close to the lake. Well, I believe you are one of those people. I believe you are in tune with the spirits of the past. What is it that Running Deer is telling you?"

"So you believe me?"

"Are you kidding? After what I've seen so far, how can I not believe you, Sierra? I mean, after seeing with my own two eyes what you can do, I have to believe you! You should be one of the X-Men or something! And you're so troubled inside; someone so beautiful shouldn't be so troubled. I don't know—it's like whatever's pulled you to be here has had a stronger grip on you than it has on anyone else I have ever met. I believe everything about this place has something to do with what's going on in your dreams and inside your head. I want to help you so badly, but…I don't know how."

"You do understand." She smiled.

"Yes, I do, Sierra. I've been studying the history if this town, the folklore, the tales that all the older residents talk about. Man, they have some doozies. It's part of my studies, but the more I read and investigate, the closer I feel with its past. And this town has such a rich past. There are so many legends in this region. If the trees and water could talk, they'd be screaming right now, because I think they feel you. You're so in tune with this place, it's really obvious. You say Running Deer has been haunting you, right?"

She nodded her head, staring out and mesmerized by the still water.

"Well, Sierra, have you ever thought that maybe there's a reason he wants you here? Why is he talking only to you and no one else here? Why are you so special to him?"

"Well, he told me he has a reason he wants me here. He needs me for something."

Tyler sat on the rock and looked up at her while holding her in soft hug.

"Okay, so what's he telling you? What's the reason?"

"I—I don't know, I saw—I saw my family. I see them a lot, Tyler. And he tricked me into thinking they were still alive just so he could get me here. That pissed me off so bad. Then Mom—she walked through a glass door and told me to ask you to bring me here, but she wasn't there. She wasn't there! Why are they doing this to me?"

She started crying, and he held her.

"Listen, this is your destiny, Sierra. Obviously you are the chosen one. Of what, I have no idea. No local legend talks about anything close to what you're telling me, but for crying out loud, Sierra, don't fight it."

They stared into each other's eyes.

"Don't fight it…"

He didn't hear that whisper; it came from the water behind him and was something only her ears caught. He stood, took her by the hand, and helped her up to the top of the rock formation.

"I want you to do something, Sierra, okay? I want you to stand at the top of that rock and close your eyes. Can you do that for me?"

"Why? Are you going to push me into the lake?"

"No, Sierra, I'd never do that, but for some reason I think you need to be at the top of the rock." He gave her a reassuring smile. "I won't leave you. I'll be right here—promise."

She stared into his eyes. He was serious, and she didn't know why.

"Okay." She breathed.

"If anything, I know that Running Deer stood on this rock, there's a painting showing it, and there's a story that he confronted soldiers here. I think you need to stand here and meditate. I won't leave your side."

He stepped by as she passed him and walked up to the top of the rock. The formation almost did look like the head of a big dog, and though the spring gushing water right underneath where they stood was a pleasant sound to the ears, the body of water called Old Indian Lake didn't look as big from the top of the rock as she had thought it would. Of course, when looking far out she didn't catch the fact that the land formation to the right that caused the boomerang shape blocked the rest of the view of the water, enough to make it look smaller from her point of view.

"Okay, so I'm up here…."

"So, relax. Chill, concentrate."

"Chatto." The word was a whisper in the soft breeze that covered her.

"Chatto," she whispered to herself. She repeated it after she heard it. "Chatto… rock. It means rock. How do I know that?"

She looked down at Tyler. He had his arms folded and

was staring at her in a reassuring smile. Her short black dress started to follow the current of the wind, which picked up after she closed her eyes again. She stood there. She felt the wind, heard the birds, and knew Tyler was standing below, watching her every move. Then she stretched out her hands. It took all of about three seconds for her to start to feel something else. There was a radiant light forming at her fingertips. She could feel it. It was warm. Then something scraped against her arm, then her forehead, then her leg. She opened her eyes, and white flakes that looked like the flames from the tip of a candle started to appear all around her. The sky grew black around them, and she was in the midst of a shower of these little flakes. Tyler started to run up to get to her.

"No, Tyler, wait," she said, and she closed her eyes again. "I'm okay. This is his energy, the energy of Running Deer, and the Great Spirit."

Tyler yanked out his cell phone and started taking video and pictures of what he saw. He knew to expect something truly extraordinary, but what he'd thought he might witness was nothing compared to this.

"Sierra, are you okay?" he called out.

She waved him off, not even turning to acknowledge him, and remained quiet, soaking in the warmth that enveloped her like a hot blanket. She opened her eyes and gazed through the flakes in front of her, and to her amazement she witnessed a bright light form around her palms. The heat from this light formed beads of sweat around her wrists. It grew into an orb that radiated at her fingertips and grew brighter, forming into the shape of a ball. Then the ball of light spread apart into a hole that opened in the air right in front of her, and she saw through the hole. Sierra quickly realized that what she saw through the open space in the air in front of her didn't coincide with what was around her. It was like viewing two TV sets side by side. Around the outside of hole was real time, but through the hole was completely something else. The trees were different, the sky was different, the time of day was different, even the color of the water didn't seem right.

"What is this? Why does it look..? Am I looking through time?"

She peered through the portal, and it seemed even the season she was witnessing didn't coincide with where she was. She turned to Tyler with a gasp. He had his phone aimed at her, though he had no clue what she was looking at. He didn't see what she saw.

Glancing back, she peered through the open crack in time, and a scene started to unfold as it took place ages ago right on the very rock where she stood. History relived itself before her eyes. It was like viewing a movie.

The tall, rugged, and confident Native American running toward her was surely none other than Running Deer, and his small band of warriors followed. Behind them, a disorganized troop of disheveled, angry men. A short hand-to-hand battle ensued, and the determined Seminoles fought hard and fought bravely, but they were no match for the men who had their sights on the big picture. Their rifles and artillery easily overpowered the crude weaponry of his Seminole tribe. There was a standstill, and Running Deer's men were circled. She saw the uniformed officer approach the warrior in the same spot where she stood. She took a step back; she felt his presence as if he were standing right next to her. Pride beamed off him like sunlight off a shiny palm leaf, but the anger of the officer radiated off him to the point that it almost scared her.

"On the order of General Andrew Jackson, I command you to vacate. You will leave this land. You will leave and never return." The man had a rifle pointed right at Running Deer. The look on his face showed that he meant business: no smile, widely opened eyes, and he spit on the ground after he made his statement.

The grimy-faced soldier didn't seem to cause the fear he had hoped in the Seminole.

"Is-tee-lock-say-tah-mas-tchay," was Running Deer's reply. They didn't understand what he said, had no idea that he had just called the man a liar.

"What did you say, redskin?" He cocked the weapon.

Running Deer, a muscular, tanned, noble warrior and holy man, had a wolf sitting at his side. Sierra and the animal locked eyes with each other. Running Deer passed his hand over the wolf's head to calm him.

He knew that Andrew Jackson had begun his war against the Indians, but he didn't know why. They had done nothing to him as far as he knew, and for the longest time they had willingly shared some of their land within the region. But this land, this very spot where they faced a stand-off, Running Deer was not willing to give up or give away, not without a fight. He also knew that the white man wanted this land for personal reasons; it was rich in soil, and for some reason the foreigners thought there was gold here or something else valuable, because the greed in their eyes shone like the rising sun on a warm summer morning. It was an unhealthy hunger he had seen before in the Spaniards who had come hundreds of years earlier. He refused to give up his home to people who didn't belong here. He wouldn't do it then and he wasn't about to do it now. Running Deer was a permanent fixture on this land. Time meant nothing to him. He drew a symbol on the sand in the rock with his spear. It resembled the letter U. The soldier looked down and stared at it.

"What? What the hell's that mean, Indian? U? Ugly? Uncle? Umbrella? Unicorn?"

The other soldiers laughed. As Sierra witnessed this, looking around at all the men surrounding her, she did a double-take and froze, concentrating on one particular soldier. She was positive she'd seen him before, he looked like…looked like…"Mr. Kettleman." She whispered.

Then the tall Seminole stepped back, stabbed his spear into the rock, and an arrow shot through the air. It flew right over Running Deer's shoulder and stabbed into the military man's chest. The brave holy man turned in anger at the warrior who had shot the arrow and pointed at him, and two other Seminole warriors grabbed him. He didn't even have time to say anything because one of the soldiers drew his weapon and shot the archer in the head. He fell to the ground, a fresh corpse. The wolf barked and leapt for the soldier with the gun drawn, landed on him, and was ready to rip him to shreds. The other soldiers drew their weapons.

"Hattis cheh!" a calm Running Deer commanded.

The wolf halted its attack but didn't close its mouth.

Its deadly salivating fangs shone brightly to everyone there. It started to growl at the soldier, who was slowly drawing his weapon at it. Running Deer passed his hand over the animal's head, stroking his fur back again.

"Yaha Hajo, Wykas-chay!" he muttered to the animal. The Americans standing there had no idea what he had said, but the Native Americans standing there and Sierra knew he said "Mad wolf, be still, quit!'"

The animal understood and listened. Unknown to the soldiers there, Running Deer had an unnatural kinship with animals. And that kinship saved one of their soldiers at that moment because the wolf craved the taste of blood and flesh and was ready to indulge. It would have no problem ripping the soldier to shreds in front of everyone there, but Running Deer didn't want to have to resort to violence if he didn't have to.

"We will not go," he muttered to the soldier in broken English. "This is our home."

"Then you will die."

"You have no right to kill us, nor the power," another of the better spoken warriors said, "The Great Spirit gives and grants power such as this. You are not of our people, and the Great Spirit does not allow you the power to take it."

The officer turned to another of his soldiers, beaming a sneer that caused them to laugh, but the Seminoles found no humor in it at all.

"Izzat so? Y'all heard him? The Great Spirit don't allow…" he sang that line back to the warrior and shook his neck in rhythm to the words.

The other soldiers chuckled under their breaths, mocking the warrior.

"Let me introduce you to my great spirit, Injun. It's called a Harper's Ferry Flintlock pistol. I loaded it just in case we were gonna have trouble, and it sure seems ta me we gots trouble, eh boys?"

He turned, drew his weapon at Running Deer, aimed, and pulled the trigger.

BLAM!

He shot the gun, but Running Deer didn't fall. Instead, the soldier who pulled the trigger fell and fell hard. The force of the shot sent him backward, where he dropped on the rock, cracked his skull on the tip of the formation's dog head, and rolled over the edge moaning in quick pain. He gurgled, trying to speak, but only blood came out of his mouth. Then they all witnessed him take the 20-foot drop into the cold abyss.

SPLASH!

"Bartholomew!" called one of the other soldiers.

The gun had exploded in his hand, and in the process blew his hand apart. A fragment of the explosion shot him in the heart; he didn't even feel the cold waters of Old Indian Lake as his body hit the surface hard and sharp. He simply splashed in, lifeless and bleeding, and quickly started to sink.

"Bart!?"

One of the soldiers dropped his weapon and jumped in the water to save his commanding officer, but it was useless, Corporal Bartholomew Simpson Page's body never rose to the surface of the water.

"You... you dad-gum Injun, you killed him with freak magic or somethin'!" screamed one of the other soldiers,

"Elijah! Kill 'em! Kill 'em all!" he ordered the other soldier.

Running Deer said nothing. He just slowly shook his head.

The soldier, along with the other two there who were left standing, drew their weapons and emptied them on the three Seminole warriors. Running Deer fell as repeated bullets zipped by, ripping through flesh, but the wolf leapt up and grabbed one of the soldiers by the face in his mighty jaws, and they both fell back over the rock and into the deep, cold waters of Old Indian Lake. That soldier's name was Elijah Jonathan Kettleman, ancestor of Wilbur. Elijah drowned, but the wolf swam to the other side. All the rest of those left fighting were killed in the skirmish that to Sierra seemed to last forever but in truth lasted only a full forty-five seconds in length. The soldiers and warriors all died, either by bullet, by arrow, or by drowning. There were no survivors of this battle, save for the wolf that safely made it to the shore but turned and faced Sierra through the hole and barked at her. The hole closed quickly, and the last thing she saw was the solemn stare of the wild animal on the shore.

* * *

Sierra stepped back and landed hard on her knees on the ground. Tyler rushed to her and grabbed her in his arms. "Sierra, are you okay? What happened? You screamed. Did you see something? And what's with all these weird flakes?"

"They killed him. Right here, Tyler! Those idiots killed him!"

"Killed who? Sierra, what's wrong? What happened? Did

you see Running Deer? Tell me! What did he say?"

She burst into tears, and he held her as they looked over the still water. The flame-like flakes softly disintegrated into the air, and the warmth around her hands from the light faded off. But she looked out while softly crying over Tyler's shoulder and could see a faded vision of Running Deer's face. It was as if only his face were in a small cloud and floating. It got closer and closer to her, to the point that she was staring in his dark eyes, and as she stared inside him through his eyes, she saw out into the panorama of the lake environment, and saw animals die, buildings take shape, a mini-mall, and cars, tractors, trucks… and smog. Then, in the instant the vision had come, it was gone.

She stared back out into the peaceful scene, and a lone wolf sat on the banks of the lake, yards away. It was staring at her. Its red eyes sparkled in the sun. It dug its paw into the sand, as if it were trying to draw something, then ran back into the woods. She pulled back from Tyler, glanced out again over the rock into the natural paradise of the beautiful lake, and her eyebrows curled down in slow anger. It finally hit her: The whole reason Running Deer was haunting her, why her family wouldn't leave her alone, and why the wolf and she were as one. Through all the questions, nightmares and tears, finally, Sierra Nora Russo got it, and she knew she had to do something about it. She knew this was her inevitable destiny.

CHAPTER SIXTEEN

Back at the cabins, Wilbur was finishing off a sandwich
and a cup of coffee when he noticed the shiny black Escalade
drive up outside. Being the overseer of the Old Indian Lake
Cabin Retreat camp for as many years as he had, he had
grown to know several things right off the bat. Usually when
a vehicle drove up it was either a family looking to book a
cabin for a family vacation, or businessmen looking for a
cheaper alternative to the hotel in downtown, or maybe an
occasional couple looking to get away for the weekend. But
the people in this huge car looked like none of the above.

The first man to step out was a tall, rugged, tanned man

with a receding hairline, a deep brow, and jaws that looked like Richard Nixon's. He adjusted his tie and opened the back door. A woman stepped out. She looked to be in her late thirties, African-American, with dark and light brown dreadlocks that went halfway down her back. She wore dark-rimmed glasses and sported firm calves that showed under the short business skirt. She had a gym membership, for sure. She almost looked like a young Halle Berry, if Halle had that kind of hair, and Wilbur, who loved Halle Berry, did a double take. She wore a matching dark blue business jacket, was holding an iPad, and wore heels that didn't seem suited for the ground she was walking on.

The other two passengers in the car walked around the vehicle and seemed to wait for her and the tall man to make their move. One of these was a thin, pale stick of a man whose suit looked like it was two sizes bigger than needed. The other, a serious go-getter type, held a briefcase and walked up behind the woman. She nodded, and they all proceeded toward the porch, where Wilbur was taking his last swig of coffee.

"Uh, might I help ya's? You shore don't look like Old Indian Lake residents, so ya's got ta be out-of-towners. Looking for a cabin for business, or..?"

The tall man reached over and handed Wilbur a shiny business card. Wilbur looked at it. The logo seemed familiar. He had seen it sprinkled on signs and billboards all over town.

"P-Mac?" he shoved it in his shirt pocket.

"Sir, this is Phyllis McMurrin, of P-Mac Developers. I'm sure you've heard about the expansion project that's slated to start soon. Some of this land here will be redeveloped for the grand hotel and office complex that will complement the convention center on the other side of the lake." The man was pointing out at the land around them as he spoke.

"I think I might have heard of it, if y'all are the same people been calling me and I've been hanging up on. Y'all don't take no for an answer very well, do ya? And I'm sure that the city council repealed that plan. You see, us natives don't want no friggin' malls and buildings put out here, furthermore..."

"Furthermore," Phyllis said stepping up to him, "... your Old Indian Lake city council just voted four to one to go ahead with this plan. Wilbur Kettleman, I'm here to propose a deal to you. P-Mac Developers is ready to pay you for your piece of land. We know the history here; your family has run this piece of land for years. But unfortunately for you, you are the last of the Kettleman line. You have no kids, your wife is dead—it stops with you. We will buy you out for two million dollars, simple, quick...."

"Think about it, old man," the tall man said in a deep, gritty tone. "...You can retire, move to Key West, and live out the rest of your days a rich man in Margaritaville. Lie back, watch the sunset every night, and maybe even get a young girlfriend to help you spend your money." He smiled.

Wilbur didn't smile back, though the mention of Key West brought a quick flashback of his first love, Suzette. She was the one he'd let get away. He married his wife, and they remained happily married for fifty-three years, but he never got over Suzette.

The man pulled a brochure out of his jacket pocket proclaiming "Welcome to Key West," reached over, and handed it to him. Wilbur read the title, turned, and looked at each of them one by one.

The tall man looked like he was a bouncer of a bike club; the pale, nervous one had to be the woman's personal secretary or accountant, and the other one, who didn't shine a smile and was constantly looking around as if he were checking to see if anyone was watching, stood maybe five foot-ten, with a thin, muscular build and had a tattoo on his hand, and wore a black suit that seemed as if it had been fitted perfectly for him by a tailor. He had slick black curly hair and almost looked like he could be related to Tom Cruise. Wilbur stared at the tattoo on his wrist but couldn't make it out.

"You know, my grandfather told me that when President Eisenhower put the highway out there, it brought more people to our town and turned this sleepy little town into a mecca for businesspeople looking for a quiet place to have meetings and conventions. Grandpa had an idea. He bought this piece of land, built these cabins, and people came. Grandpa was a visionary, and his dream is still alive today." He looked at the back of the Key West flier.

"That's true, Mr. Kettleman." Phyllis smiled. "Your grandfather was a true visionary. You know, people like him are what make America work. The lazy good-for-nothings sit back and complain, but people like your grandfather get what the true ingenuity of the great American spirit is all about. I share that with him. It's something I got from my dad."

"Like what, buying out people's happiness? You are what makes capitalism a bad word, Miss Thing." Wilbur hacked.

"Look, old man…." the tall enforcer started.

Phyllis patted his hand. He stepped back, fuming.

Wilbur stepped forward. "Well, you know what? Nobody here in Old Indian Lake asked President Eisenhower to put that cursed highway out there. 'Oh yeah,' they said, 'it's going to bring more jobs to your sleepy little town.' Yeah, it did, till they finished the highway and kept going down the line and took the workers with 'em. Then they forgot about us. Well, you know what, Miss Phyllis? Us natives, we were happy being a sleepy little town, and I don't like what the highway's done to Old Indian Lake, and I sure as hell don't intend to just give you my land here for you to mess it up, no ma'am!"

"You're not giving it to us; you're selling it to us, Kettleman," the briefcase man screamed.

"No—actually I'm not sellin' it. You can take your two million and shove it where the sun don't shine, Sonny, and lady why don't you go build in in another town? Try Danica, or Lobo Cliff, or Aston, Cobra Lake… or even DeLeon Beach! We Old Indian Lakers don't want 'cha here. We don't want change, we don't want no fancy-schmancy hotel, or a rebuilt convention center. What's next—a casino? For Pete's sake!"

"Now, you're making a big mistake, Mr. Kettleman."

"Yep, ya got that right, young man. My mistake was that I shoulda told you to skedaddle when I first saw ya drive up in that there mini-tank. Now go on."

"We want this land, Mr. Kettleman. The whole deal with this town depends on the acquisition of this property. Okay, look, how about two and a half mil, plus I will grant you a lifetime membership to the hotel that we will build here. So whenever you come back home, you'll have a king suite to stay in with top of the line everything in it. We will even name it the Kettleman Suite, in honor of your family. Now admit it, you can't get any better than that. Your grandfather—rest his soul—would be proud of that." Phyllis forced a smile.

Wilbur took two steps down the wooden staircase to meet her face-to-face.

"Whadda ya say, old man?" the man with the briefcase asked.

Wilbur dropped the Key West brochure on the ground in front of them.

"Let me spell it for ya," he grunted. "N–O."

She caught a whiff of his tobacco- and coffee-stained breath and stepped back.

"Sir, I d-d-don't think you understand the g-g-gravity of this acquisition," the pale one stammered. "You s-s-stand to make a k-k-killing with this d-d-deal."

"Yeah," the one holding the briefcase added. "You're the last of your line, Kettleman. Think this over. It would be a shame if anything should happen to you. What would happen to this precious land of yours?"

"It's being given to someone in my will."

"Who?" Phyllis asked. It was evident by the expression on her face that she was surprised at this information.

"That, ma'am, is none of your dadgum beeswax! Now take your three musketeers here and hightail it before I bring out my Louisville Slugger and open up some skulls. I played baseball back in the day. Don't think I won't."

"Look, old timer!" The tall man grabbed Wilbur by the collar.

"Frank!" Phyllis snapped.

The tall man turned to her.

"Let him go. He has free will to make his decisions. If he doesn't want to sign over the land to us, there are other ways to take care of this. We're businesspeople. We'll do it my way."

The husky Frank let thin, frail Wilbur go, then wiped his hands. "I'll see you again, old man." He pointed at him and stressed every word with his finger.

Wilbur straightened out his shirt.

"No ya won't, Lurch."

The pale one was already walking back to the Escalade. It was obvious that either the sun or the confrontation, or maybe both, were bothering him.

"Excuse me, may I use your bathroom before we leave?" the briefcase man asked.

"Sure, right in there, first door to the left of the office. Says restroom. You can read, right?"

Phyllis walked up to Wilbur and helped straighten out his collar.

"I apologize for the actions of my associate. This is not how we do business. I take pride in my work, and I am sure we can come to an agreement. I will make sure that you receive the best that I can give. I will have my lawyer contact your lawyer."

"I don't have a lawyer, lady. Don't need one. Never have, 'cept for my will. My answer is a flat out no—that's a capital N and a capital O. Want me to write it in the sand for ya? Ya city slickers don't understand, a hick town as y'all call it, is considered paradise to some folk. You wantin' ta turn this into another Tampa or Miami or Jacksonville just so you can capitalize on our name is gonna kill Old Indian Lake. And you don't even care. This here town is about people, honey, not money!"

She turned. "Have a nice day, Mr. Kettleman," she coldly uttered under her breath. Frank opened the door for her.

The footsteps behind him in the cabin signaled to Wilbur that the other associate was on his way out. He hopped off the porch after shoving open the wooden screen door, patted the caretaker on the back, and walked off to the car.

"Later, old timer." He smiled. "Say hi to the wife for me."

Walter stepped back on the porch and watched the huge, shiny black SUV back out and speed away. He stared at the logo on the side door.

"P-Mac. Phooey!" He spat across the sand.

v v v v v v

Up the road, the Harley-Davidson was speeding back from the spring. Sierra held on tightly to Tyler, buried her face into his back, and sighed. Standing on that rock had done something to her. She felt different now. Whether she liked it or not, something had changed. She had a purpose, a meaning, she understood. Finally she felt at one with her surroundings. And Tyler now felt a closer kinship with Sierra. Sure, he was attracted to her anyway, but he also felt for some reason he had to protect her. He didn't want to leave her side, and he didn't know why. They turned the corner and were within viewing distance of the cabins.

"Hey Sierra, wanna go see Wilbur?"

"Sure." She smiled. "You know, I love that old ma—"

KA-BLOOOM!

The force of the explosion from Wilbur's cabin caught the two onlookers totally by surprise.

"Oh God!"

"Mr. Kettleman!"

Tyler punched it and sped down to the cabin site. The door to one of the guest cabins burst open, and a woman ran out toward the fire to witness the fury. Wilbur Kettleman's cabin was engulfed in flame.

"Hurry, Tyler, hurry!" Sierra screamed.

In no time the Harley skidded to a halt near the tool shed. He ran toward the burning building. The woman was on her cell calling 911. Tyler rushed for the hose on the side of Wilbur's cabin, but the flames kept him at a distance. Sierra instead ran toward the shoreline and stared out.

"Yes, there was an explosion at Old Indian Lake Cabin Retreat!" the woman screamed on her cell. "There's a fire. Please hurry!"

The heat was already unbearable, but Tyler yanked off his shirt, covered his hand with it, reached for the spigot, and turned. A gush of water flowed out but quickly went down to a trickle.

"What? Nooo!" he screamed, "Wilbur!"

Sierra stood at the shoreline and stared out into the vast lake. She tried to remain calm but she was fidgeting all over. "Running Deer, help me. I need you!" she screamed.

"Sierra…"The whisper calmed her. She raised her right hand with her eyes closed, then turned it in the air like she was turning on an invisible faucet. The water in the lake started to gurgle.

"Tyler, move away from the cabin!" she screamed.

"What?"

"Move away!"

She shoved her hand toward the burning building and a wave of water flew into the air, headed for the cabin.

"Oh… I see," he said. Tyler dropped the hose and ran toward the tool shed.

In seconds the huge wave engulfed the burning building and put out the fire in one fell swoop.

"What the…?" the woman dropped her cell phone.

The 911 operator was still audible. "Hello, ma'am, hello? Fire department is on their way…. Hello?"

As soon as the water washed away and drew itself back into the lake, Tyler ran up the stairs and kicked his way though the half-shattered door.

"Wilbur! Wilbur, are you in here?"

Sierra ran in behind him. "Mr. Kettleman, please answer us!" It took only a second for her to find him, on the floor across the room, badly burned and soaked. "Oh God!"

Tyler shoved over the file cabinet and knelt to him. "Wilbur, are you all right?"

He didn't move. Tyler touched his throat. He felt no pulse. "Oh no...." He covered his face in his hands and started to cry.

"Sierra... he's...."

"No! No! Don't say it, no!"

The woman with the cell phone ran in. "Is Mr. Kettleman all right?"

Tyler stood up, shook his head.

"Oh my word. I called 911. They're on their way."

"It's too late, too late."

Sierra bent down to Wilbur. Something was sticking out of his shirt pocket. She pulled it out—a half-burned business card. "P-Mac Development. I've seen this logo. It's posted all over town," she said, wiping her eyes.

Tyler looked at it. "Yeah, those are the people who want to basically buy the town out. They want to build high-rises and hotels and parking garages. They're the ones who want to give your uncle that big job here. In fact, they got into an argument with old man Crabtree, who owns the gas station. Then ironically he died in a car accident the next day."

"Mighty convenient, don't you think?" Sierra said.

"Yeah, I heard the sheriff say they wanted to buy this campsite and build something here."

"That must be who was here visiting. I saw that logo on a

huge Escalade that was here just a few minutes ago." the lady said, staring at the card.

"They were here?"

The emergency vehicle sirens approached in the distance.

"Yeah, my husband and I were in our cabin—we're the only ones here right now—and four people came out of the car and were talking to Mr. Kettleman. He was such a nice man. He didn't seem to be too pleased with them. I wanted to come out and see what was going on, but my husband tells me I'm always in other people's business. 'Sara, stop getting all up in other people's business' he's always saying."

"Well, Miss Sara, for once you can tell your husband that I said thank you for getting in someone else's business, because now we know who killed Mr. Kettleman, and I'm not going to let this go. Tyler come on—we have to pay a visit to P-Mac."

The sheriff's car swerved outside and stopped at the smoldering building. Smoke was billowing high off the burned and watered down frame. Sierra and Tyler were walking out.

"What in the blazes?"

The aging sheriff stepped out of his cruiser, and the deputy with him ran inside the building.

"Sheriff, do you know where I can find these people?" Sierra asked angrily shoving the half business card in his face.

He stepped back, gave her a once-over. "Young lady, who do you think…hey, ain't you Sierra Russo? Joe and Tina's baby? You know I thought I saw Nelson here yesterday. Y'all staying in town? Why, I remember the day you were born…"

"This is important, Sheriff," Tyler added.

"Huh? Oh, okay, well, uh, yeah, P-Mac. Them dad-gum developers are getting on my nerve. They're going to ruin this town. I'm thinking twice about the offer they gave me. Feels kinda slimy. Anyway, they have a trailer over on Gadsden Boulevard. Somebody wanna tell me exactly what happened here? Fire truck's gonna be here any minute and I don't even think we need 'em now."

"They did this. They blew up his cabin and killed Mr. Kettleman, and I'm going after them."

She rushed by him, and he reached out and grabbed her arm and pulled her back.

"Whoa now, girl, what do you mean they did this? Do you have proof that they did this? You're talking about a huge corporation, now."

"I don't care how big they are, Sheriff. They killed the one man who believed my story and knew my history. This Phyllis lady? She's mine."

"Sierra honey, I understand your anger, but you just can't go accusing people."

Sara's husband was walking out toward them right when the deputy stepped out of the burned cabin. "Wilbur's dead, Sheriff," the young deputy stated. "It don't look good in there."

"Dead? Now wait a minute…."

"I just told you they killed him!" Sierra fumed.

Sara, the onlooker, stepped up to him. "Sheriff, those developers came here, had an argument with him, then they left, and his cabin blew up. I saw it with my own two eyes."

"Sara, stay out of this. Stop getting in people's business," her husband started.

"Benjamin, shut up," she said.

"Them's serious allegations, now. Are you sure it was them?"

"Sheriff, if you need me as a witness, I will witness. Mr. Kettleman was a nice man, and he didn't deserve this. This retreat was his life. This just isn't fair!"

The sheriff turned to his deputy and sighed. "Bubba, get in the car. We need to go pay a visit."

"Sheriff, I'm coming with you."

"No, Sierra, you're not. This is official police business."

He walked around and got in the passenger seat.

"Tyler, get the bike." Sierra said. She walked over to the car and rapped her fingers on the hood, creating a rhythmic drum beat all her own, then turned away.

The ambulance and then the fire truck finally arrived and parked right behind the sheriff's car. Tyler revved up the Harley and rode slowly over to Sierra, who hopped on. The deputy turned the car on, and immediately it started to overheat. The water in the radiator turned to steam, and the car stalled.

"What the..?"

Tyler rode off as Sierra waved and smiled. "Bye, Sheriff."

The sheriff hopped out of the car and threw his hat on the ground.

CHAPTER SEVENTEEN

They rode in silence, with different things on their minds. Tyler was consumed with the amazing girl riding on his bike just behind him, holding him tightly as they zoomed down the winding dirt road. Try as he might, he couldn't shake the feelings he was starting to have about the mysterious teenage beauty who, although a native of his hometown, had been raised in St. Pete, away from the history of her horrid past.

She, although holding on to him as the bumpy road and swift ride gave her time to think, couldn't shake all the emotions swimming in her mind, but of all of them two stood prominent: rage and vengeance. They were swelling in her brain like an angry cancer, and the anger grew the longer it took to get there. Wilbur Kettleman wasn't just a resident; he was the face of Old Indian Lake to any visitor who came for a peaceful, relaxing vacation away from it all, and in one selfish deed, a corporation—or at least the person in charge of the corporation—had erased him from the face of the earth. That wasn't fair, and she wasn't about to let it go.

Aside from her family, Sierra had never known anyone else who died, but she had gotten to know Wilbur Kettleman, had come to love and respect the man. Watching him snuffed from life was going to be just another hurdle for her to have to deal with—but that would have to wait. Because now she finally got it; it all hit her like a trailer full of bricks.

What the ghosts of her family and what the old Seminole medicine man meant by "a war is coming." The war the whispers from the soothing lake and the voices of the lost souls in and around Old Indian Lake were clamoring for. It wasn't war as in a fight with weapons and artillery, no—it was a war for the precious land that Running Deer died for. She had turned her back on Running Deer, she said no to the ghosts of her departed family, she ignored the whispers from the lake—but today, today the residents of Old Indian Lake, Florida had just gotten a new warrior on their side.

No, P-Mac was not going to build in Old Indian Lake— not if Sierra Nora Russo had any say-so about it. And she knew this time she did have a say-so.

They both were concentrating on their own issues when

they heard the siren behind them. Tyler looked in his rear-view mirror.

"Oh crap."

He slowed down and pulled over, and the deputy's car pulled up close behind him. The door opened, and a middle-aged overweight deputy stepped out of the driver's side, a younger African-American deputy hopped out the other side and quickly stepped up to the Harley. "Hey Tyler, 'sup?"

"Jake, what's going on? Was I going too fast?"

"Uh, nah, but—well, the sheriff radioed us and told us to uh…detain you."

Tyler and Sierra shared quick glances at each other. "Detain me? What did I do?"

"Tyler Phillips, the sheriff tells me that you and your girlfriend here are out to do no good uptown. Now, you wanna tell me what exactly is going on here?"

Head deputy Sam Cunningham was a bear of a man; he adjusted his belt and spit tobacco across the street. His uniform seemed a size too small as did his hat, and he didn't look like he was in a good mood, either. The frown on his face gave that away. Being head deputy of a small town means you know people, almost all the people of your town by name and family, and he'd known Tyler since Tyler was born.

"Sam, we didn't do anything. Did he tell you that Wilbur got killed?"

"Well yeah, he told me that Wilbur died in a freak fire—"

"It wasn't a freak fire!" Sierra spat. "It was arson! It was murder! They killed him!"

"Young lady, you don't go accusing people, especially Miss Phyllis McMurrin, of something like murder unless you have concrete evidence, and even with evidence you need to—"

"What the hell is it with you people?" She hopped off the bike. "Is she paying the city millions to do it her way? Are you on her payroll or something? She must have offered each and every one of you morons something and you people are only seeing dollar signs! She killed Wilbur Kettleman, she probably killed the gas station owner—doesn't that mean anything to you at all? These people are your neighbors, your friends! Phyllis is a cold-blooded, ruthless witch! Don't you even see that?" she was in his face and pointing her finger in his chest.

"Now, young lady, I suggest that you calm down and go on back home and—"

"I am home, Jethro! And I'm not going to let those jerks destroy my home or my people! This is war; if you're not going to do anything about it, then go back to the Donut Hut and stay out of my way! Come on, Tyler."

"Tyler Phillips, don't get back on that bike," the deputy ordered.

"Aw come on, Sam," Tyler reasoned.

"I'm serious, boy. You gointa get yourself in a heap of trouble if you defy me."

Tyler looked at the younger deputy. They were close friends.

"Jake?"

"Dude, he's my boss. I can't help ya."

"Fine! I'll walk." Sierra fumed.

She started off up the road alone. Tyler walked over to his bike.

"Tyler Phillips, you get on that bike, I swear to crimony I'll call your grandma Karen and tell her that you're aiding in a felony. Now you just got that big scholarship. You don't wanna mess that up, do ya? Well, do ya?"

"Felony? Sam we're just going up to see that Phyllis lady!"

"The look on that girl's face says a lot more than a friendly visit to say hello and trade recipes, son."

"She's feisty!" the young deputy added in a smile. An angry glance from Sam quickly wiped the grin off his face.

Tyler got on his bike. "I'm sorry, Sam, but I have to go with her on this. I believe they killed Wilbur, and if they'll kill an old man to get his land, and Crabtree for his gas station property, what will they do to a teenage girl who is going to fight and stand up to them? You're an officer of the law; you should be on her side, because you took an oath to uphold the law. I don't know about you, but I'm backing her up, and I'm not letting her go up there alone."

"I'm with him, Sam." The young officer said, getting back in the car.

"Jake, I ain't ask for your opinion."

"All the same, Sam, we should follow them up there. Never know what can happen. If something happens to Tyler, whoo boy, Miss Karen'll be on you like stink on cow manure."

Tyler started his Harley and scooted up to meet with Sierra, then looked back at Sam, who was scratching his head in frustration. He turned back to his young partner, who was motioning for him to get in the car.

"Aw hell, Jake." He walked back to the car.

v v v v v v

The office of P-Mac Developers was busy. Though they were packed in a small trailer right near the creek, Phyllis McMurrin and her underlings were busily working on documents to fulfill their plans. Her mobile office was command central, and whenever they sought to take over a new location, they'd pack the mobile office and drive it to the intended place, park it on a rented lot, and go to work. Phyllis was a multi-millionaire who had gotten where she did by making daring moves in the business and real estate worlds. And she did everything she could to make it to the top. She had first seen the opportunity in the small town of Old Indian Lake when she came to a seminar once and was taken by how folksy the town was, but she had vision and she knew she could make it happen, despite the odds. And her odds were to fight with residents of this town who refused change.

She'd been through this before, many times. It was no real challenge—just another region and another method. All she had to do was present it the right way to the city council, and she'd dealt with local government entities most of her career. They were putty in her hands. You offer them the right amount of money, assure a spike in job growth and revenue for the community, ask for certain tax incentives, and show your past projects that have bloomed into major money-making enterprises—and the proposition was as good

as done. She knew the game very well. She was a master. The
tall man walked into her office. The frown on his face seemed
to be glued on.

"Ms. McMurrin, this just got faxed to us. It seems the
old man was telling the truth. The campsite is indeed willed
to someone else, and—get this—the person don't even live
here. I can send Justin to go out and investigate who exactly
this person is, in fact, it doesn't say if it's a family member or
not."

"I researched Wilbur Kettleman. He has no family,
Frank. His wife passed away years ago, and they had no
kids, nephews, or nieces. That's why he was easy to wipe off;
no one will come looking for him. He was just collateral
damage." She reached out for the paper and read as he
continued.

"Well, it seems that the whole campsite property will be
turned over to some girl named Sierra Russo. And, ma'am,
she's a minor."

"A minor? Ha, that will be easy. Let's see," she rubbed
her chin and stared out the window to the road. "I'm sure
she probably doesn't even have an attorney, so a trip to
Disney World for a week—all expenses paid, of course, and
at a five-star resort. Offer to cover all college expenses in the
form of a scholarship named after her town or after Wilbur
if she wants, a brand new state-of-the-art sports car when
she comes of age, trip to New York City or Hollywood—ha!
What girl doesn't want that? And throw in a little spending
spree at the mall of her choice. This is going to be a piece
of cake. What would a teenager want with an old rundown
wooden cottage campsite? Ha! This deal is all but sealed."

Phyllis grinned. "I love my job!"

The briefcase holder walked in holding a cell phone.

"Ms. McMurrin, ma'am—uh, it's the sheriff." He handed her the phone.

"Hello, Phyllis McMurrin. Oh hi, Sheriff, how's your day going? Are you getting ready for that fishing trip that P-Mac is sending you on next week? Huh? Oh you say someone has died? Wilbur Kettlebaum…oh Kettleman? No—never heard of him. What happened to him, Sheriff?" She turned to Frank and rolled her eyes. "Oh my, that's terrible, Sheriff, a fire? Does he have any family? No, I don't think I know him, oh… well come to think of it, you're right, maybe that was the man we just went to see about the property. That campsite would be a great addition to the new complex in the plans, but he nixed it. No hard feelings. We left. He wasn't in the mood to talk—that is, if this is the same older gentleman I'm thinking. Stained teeth, overalls? Yes, he turned us down but you know how business goes—win some, lose some, right? Okay, Sheriff, if we can help in any way, please let me know. I'm sure it's such a terrible tragedy for the town. I bet he was a well-liked man. Thank you. Talk to you tomorrow."

She clicked off the phone and handed it back to the briefcase man and turned back toward the window.

"Hmm." She sighed.

"Miss McMurrin, is something wrong?"

She was tapping her finger on her chin, then turned to Frank. "It seems that there was a witness at the campsite. It wasn't empty like we thought. Tonight I want you to go take care of it."

"Yes ma'am."

"W-w-what do we do about this t-t-teenager?" the accountant asked.

Phyllis McMurrin stood and looked back out the window.

"We find her, and then we strike a deal. We offer her a bargain that she can't refuse, right?" She smiled, and the men one by one started laughing along with her.

As she finished her comment, she heard the familiar roar of a Harley Davidson approaching. "Are we expecting company?"

"No ma'am, not that I know of."

She walked over to the door. "Come on."

Phyllis stepped outside, followed by her two main henchmen. As she walked out on the porch, the motorcycle coasted to a halt. Sierra hopped off before Tyler could come to a complete stop, and she ran up to the trailer where the three figures loomed on the porch.

"Phyllis McMurrin?" she asked.

"That's me, and you are...?"

"Lady, I'm going to be your worse nightmare."

"Oh really?" she smiled.

Frank stepped up and blocked her from Phyllis. His entire chest area was bigger than anything she'd seen before on a man. Sierra walked right up to him, unfazed. "Get out of my way, goon. This is between me and the boss lady."

"Sierra, back off." Tyler said, walking up to them.

"Sierra? Is your name Sierra Russo?" Phyllis asked.

"Yes."

They stared at each other through the massive biceped

arm of the enforcer between them.

"Do you know Wilbur Kettleman?" the teenager asked pointing.

"Kettleman? Kettleman, hmm, no, I can't say that I do."

"Of course you do. You just killed him!"

The three stared around at each other. Tyler had just come up behind her, and the deputy's car was parking up the drive.

"Excuse me? Killed? Young lady did you just accuse me of…?"

"Yes I did, and you'll be spending time in prison before you can start construction in this town, lady."

Frank's already-angry face managed to sour even more as he stared down on the girl. He got in Sierra's face. "Look, kid, make sure you can prove something before you go pointing fingers, before making accusations you might just wanna—"

"Get out of my face, Frankenstein." She went to walk around him, and he blocked her with one hand, then grabbed her arm, and his squeeze started to hurt. Deputy Sam stepped out of the car, lifted his cap, and walked over to them.

Sierra looked up into the man's face. "Mister, if you don't let go of my arm, you're going to regret this."

"I am, am I?" he said sarcastically, chuckling. "What are you going to do? Hit me with your purse?"

Sam walked up to the porch behind her. Sierra frowned and glared angrily into the man's eyes. Their eyes locked, and she didn't blink.

"You know, Frankenstein, the human body is…what?

Sixty percent water? What do you think would happen if that water suddenly evaporated?"

"What are you talking about, kid? I suggest you step back off this porch or I'll have to help you do just that. Do you need my help to step off the porch? Do ya, young lady? The deputy is my witness you're harassing my boss."

The man looked like an ex-pro wrestler whose business suit didn't quite fit because of his bulging arms and throat muscles.

"Ha, do you think your size scares me, Bigfoot?"

The man squeezed her arm tighter.

"Sierra, don't," Tyler whispered.

"Sir, why don't you let the girl go?" Sam started.

The man reached out his other hand. He was about to grab her other arm. She never stopped her dark, concentrated stare into his eyes; then she yanked her other arm away before he could touch it, opened up her palm, and aimed her hand at him. He grunted in anger for a second. It looked like he was in no mood for a rebellious teenager, but then he stopped, and his eyes grew wide. Those standing there weren't sure if it was shock or pain, but Tyler and Sierra knew. It was the look of pain, the kind of pain that started somewhere inside the body and was looking for a way out.

"Sierra, stop," Tyler whispered.

The man let go of her arm and buckled down, grabbing his throat. His stare into the teenage girl changed from rage to pain; then he fell helpless to his knees in front of her.

"Feeling pain, Frankenstein?" Sierra smirked.

He fell on his face coughing. Sierra stepped on him, then over him to get to Phyllis.

"Now, Ms. Phillis P-Mac, or whatever it is that you call yourself, we need to talk. We need to clear the air, understand? And we're going to do it right here in front of law enforcement. You are going to confess to murder; then your company will pack up and high-tail it out of Old Indian Lake forever, or I swear on the fresh corpse of Wilbur Kettleman, they'll have to drag you out of here in a body bag! Today isn't going to be your day."

The man on the floor passed out. Sierra closed her hand and stopped because she knew he'd die if she let it go on. The other man stepped up from behind Phyllis and drew a weapon.

"I don't know what you did to him with your freak magic, girlie, but you won't stop a bullet."

Senior Deputy Sam Cunningham's training kicked in when he saw the snub-nose weapon drawn. He grabbed Sierra's arm and shoved her to the side and into Tyler's arms. "Drop your weapon, young man!"

The rookie standing on the dirt just feet away behind him froze in shock. The face of the man with the weapon showed his impatience. He raised his gun and fired.

BLAM!

Sam fell back and on top of the rookie deputy. They both fell hard to the dirt ground.

"No! Sam!" Sierra screamed. Her scream coincided with a burst from inside the trailer, and every water receptacle attached to the building exploded. People inside the trailer were running out the door screaming in fright, and some were jumping out of windows.

"What the..?" Phyllis turned as her staff were hurriedly

rushing by her and running out into the street.

The man with the gun turned and aimed it at Sierra. "Justin, put the gun down," his boss ordered.

"No!"

"Justin!"

Sierra, Tyler, and the young deputy could see the instant confusion in his eyes. What they didn't know was that Justin Scott was an ex-con recently out of prison, and Phyllis had hired him and Frank as muscle to convince customers to see things the P-Mac way. She knew that Justin was unstable, however, and at this point, he seemed totally out of her control. And Phyllis was usually in control. But she had to try to save face.

"Justin, this isn't how we conduct ourselves in a business environment! P-Mac has principle. Put down your—"

"Screw you, McMurrin! This girl ain't seeing it our way, and I'll just have to make her see, just like I did that old man at the campsite and the geezer at the gas station. That's what you told me to do, and I did it, and this stupid teenybopper ain't gonna ruin our takeover!"

He shone a crazy grin at Sierra and pulled the trigger.

BLAM!

Sierra jumped back on top of Tyler.

"Sierra!"

But instead of Sierra suffering a bullet wound, it was her attacker who did, at the hands of Sam Cunningham, who shot him on the arm from the ground where he lay. The gun flew out of Justin's hand and landed on the wooden stairs. Sierra, now full of rage, jumped him, and they both went straight for the window and crashed through. Sierra landed on top of him, and he slapped her across the face. She fell back against the desk, then tumbled to the floor. Water was flowing all over the place. He grabbed his aching arm with the bullet wound, pulled back his hand and saw blood, then reached in the desk next to him and yanked out another pistol.

Sierra shot him an angry, frustrated stare, and water rose in front of him and formed into the shape of a huge fist, then connected full and hard across his face. He fell back and rolled over on the wet floor. Sierra, down on her knees, quickly got to her feet, staring him down. But Justin was a fighter, and this was his fight now. As far as he was concerned, girl or no girl, she was going down. Shaking in uncontrolled rage, he jumped to his feet, smiled, and aimed the gun. "You freak of nature. I'll show you to mess with Justin B. Scott!"

"Justin, stop!" Phyllis screamed from outside.

Sierra looked down at his feet and opened her palm. The water he was standing on quickly froze and became a slick surface, too slick for him to keep his balance. He struggled but proved no match and slipped, fell, and slammed his head against the chair on his way down to the floor.

CRASH!

Adrenaline forced him to move again, but Sierra leapt over and swiftly kicked him across the face. He fell back with a hard crunch to the floor. Sierra's stare into the water on the floor around him caused the water to freeze again and held him there, stuck against his will. This time Justin Scott, P-Mac enforcer and ex-con, was out of his league. Sierra hopped on top of him and started punching him on the face and chest until Tyler ran in to pull her off of him. Justin lay there panting heavily, glued to the floor and screaming obscenities at the beautiful teen.

"Sierra, are you okay?" Tyler held her in a close hug.

"Yeah." She opened both palms wide and stared around the room, and all the spigots and the water cooler, from which water was gushing out inside the small building, stopped flowing.

"Yeah, I think everything is going to be okay now. But we gotta get Sam to the clinic." She smiled.

They walked back outside, where Jake was putting cuffs on Phyllis. Sam was still lying on the ground, moaning in pain from the bullet wound.

"Tyler, help me up."

"Miss P-Mac," the young officer said, "I believe you have a lot of explaining to do to the sheriff when you get into town."

"Phyllis," Frank called weakly from the floor, "don't tell them anything."

Sierra stepped over him and faced her enemy.

"Like I said, today isn't going to be your day. Justin just confessed to murdering both men, and he shot a cop! He's in your employ. You're going down, girl."

Phillis glanced calmly at her, then at Tyler. The smirk on her face wasn't what Sierra expected.

"Young man, are you willing to give up the full scholarship that P-Mac gave you for research and school, because your girlfriend here wants to play Rambo?"

Sierra moved to face him.

"What?"

He shied away with a grimace.

"Tyler, is this true? She bought you too?"

"My grandma can't afford the schooling. It was going to be my way to realize my dream, Sierra."

"That's right," Phyllis said, smiling, "and if I go down, he loses out. So does the sheriff, so does Hoss here, who's lying on the ground, as well as the mayor, city council members.... Honey, I own this town. Uh, Hoss, tell your mini-me to take these handcuffs off me."

Sam stared at her, holding his chest, then glanced over at Sierra.

"Sam if you un-cuff her I'll report you," the teenager said.

"To whom?" Phyllis smiled devilishly. "Little girl, you don't seem to understand. Money talks, I have a grand plan, and it's going to work. I don't need these small-time hoods or those temp-for-a-day paper pushers over there working under me. I'm the boss. I'm the star. No one is going to talk against me."

Several of her employees still standing at the edge of the street fidgeted on that last comment.

"I'll go against you," Tyler said. He took Sierra by the hand.

"S-s-so will I," her bashful accountant chimed in.

Hands went up as she looked at her staff, then she turned to Sierra, fuming.

"Well, Ms. P-Mac, I guess you're not all that."

"Phyllis McMurrin, you have the right to remain silent.

Anything you say can and will be used against you," the rookie started.

"Frank, call my lawyer."

Frank flipped her the bird from the floor.

The deputy walked her to the car, finishing off his speech. Tyler and Sierra rushed down to see if they could help Sam up.

"No, never mind. Leave me here. The ambulance is on the way."

"I'm sorry, Sam. We all should have known better," Tyler told him.

"You're right, boy. Thank heaven for this little girl."

They stood, and Tyler held her in a hug.

"Well, there goes my scholarship."

"Y-y-yeah, and my r-r-raise," the accountant said, walking away.

"You did the right thing, Tyler. This town is worth it. Deep down inside, you know it." Sierra smiled. She kissed him on the cheek, and they walked away toward the Harley.

CHAPTER EIGHTEEN

It was a familiar smell to all who were gathered; some are used to it more than others. Others would rather not smell it at all, for whatever reason they choose: the ever-present smell of hospital.

"Looks like he's going to be okay. Yes indeedy." That was the unmistakable voice of Nurse Marjeanette Clinton.

Tyler rushed to the bedside. "Sam? Sam can you hear me?"

Deputy Sam Cunningham opened his eyes. "Argh, man, what hit me?" He coughed right after he said that.

"Mr. Cunningham, you just lie down now. Don't go trying to get up." The nurse placed her hand on his chest and softly pushed him back down.

He looked up at her. "Marjeanette? What the... how did I get here?"

"I brought you, sir," Jake spoke up.

"I... I was shot."

"Yes sir, and thank God that old bulletproof vest still works, though I think we're going to have to get you a new one. It was the devil trying to get it off you." The nurse chuckled.

Tyler reached up and took the deputy's huge hand in his in a hearty shake. "You saved Sierra, Sam. I'm never going to forget that. She'd have been killed if you hadn't jumped in."

"And Phyllis confessed to the killing of Wilbur. It was a sick plot," the sheriff said from the other side of the room. "So all that renovation and building in Old Indian Lake won't happen, and us natives want to keep it that way. Deep down inside we all knew it. I guess I owe Sierra an apology. In fact, the whole dad-gum town does. The girl is so in tune with the nature around this town, it's amazing. Its like the trees, the water, everything talks to her. It's just weird, Sam, ya know?"

Sam nodded in agreement as Marjeanette checked his IV.

"Yes indeed, that Sierra is one special girl," the nurse said, walking out of the room. "Sheriff, you're all going to have to leave the room and let Sam get his rest. Too much activity in this small town the past couple of days."

"Aw hell, Marjeanette, I need to get some answers here."

"Sheriff, answers are going to have to wait until he gets

better. Now come on, all of you—scoot."

Tyler put his arms around Marjeanette's shoulder and walked out into the hallway with her.

"Miss Marjeanette, when you get off work, I'm taking you out to dinner. You don't mind riding on the back of my Harley, do you?"

"Oh go on now, Tyler, you take that pretty girl out to dinner instead, okay?"

"I don't know. I'm going to look like some kinda guy with two lovely women on either side of me when I walk into Teddy's Bar-B-Que Shack." He winked.

She smacked his butt. "Boy, get out of here. Don't make me call your grandma."

"Sheriff, where's Sierra?" the downed senior officer asked.

"She's out on the patio. I'll send her in later. You get your rest, Sam. I'm going to the jail and get more answers out of this Phyllis lady. She was really shaken, it seems. I guess the lady has never lost anything in her life—and she lost big this time."

"Yeah, and to a little hick town. It must be eatin' her up—ha!"

"Yep. You get better, Sam. I'll mosey on back later."

* * *

Outside, the small clinic had a patio that overlooked a creek. The many creeks in Old Indian Lake came from the lake one way or another. This one followed a crooked trail from the southernmost tip of the lake across the western side of town and slithered behind the schoolyard, the Marathon

Gas station, and eventually the clinic, and went on for some miles. All the land that it touched seemed frozen in time. It all looked like an untouched piece of nature from a postcard picture. The wooden deck of the clinic stretched out to where a larger part of the creek trickled underneath. Its planked deck followed the creek line all the way around. The very back was a break area that was accessible through sliding glass doors. Usually it was used as the smoking area for staff and visitors. Today there was no one out there, no one but Sierra, who was alone, taking in the warm Florida sun and listening to nature at its best. As she stared at the creek, minnows swam by, and a deer peeked out of the brush to take a quiet sip. She stood still, knowing that one sound would spook it.

The solemn fifteen-year-old leaned against the railing and stared into the water. On the other side of the brook, as she glared out at the Spanish moss-filled oak trees and palm shrubs that filled the wooded area, a mist slowly rose out of the creek just to the other side of her across the water. The mist gradually formed into shapes, the familiar shapes of her family members. One by one they began to materialize right before her eyes: first her father, Joe, then her mother, Tina, then her baby sister, Breanna. She sighed a warm smile.

"Honey, I'm so proud of you." It was almost a whisper, but she heard it and recognized the voice.

"Thank you, Mom."

"We knew we could count on you, Sis." Breanna smiled.

Then out of the creek rose a shape in water form that began to take the shape of a man. His features began to mold right in front of her eyes. The arrangement of head, face, nose, shoulders sharpened like someone was molding it out of clay. Tall, dark, solemn, a form that commanded respect and attention.

"Running Deer," she gasped in a whisper.

"You did well, my daughter. My spirit can now rest, the troubled energy of lives past can rest, and the Great Spirit commends you. Continue your work. Your home needs you."

"Yes, Running Deer. And… I'm sorry."

"I am sorry means regret. You have no reason for regrets, my child. The atonement of your actions wipes you of any regret. You are family. You belong."

She smiled, and she could almost see a hint of smile from him—almost.

"Honey, we have to go, but we will always be watching over you."

"Somehow I know that, Daddy." She couldn't fight the tears that she knew were building.

"Sierra, is that cute guy with the motorcycle your boyfriend?"

"Shut up Breanna!"

She smiled, and her family did, too. Running Deer finally couldn't hold his seriousness and chuckled. Although she didn't know the language, she was speaking to them in the Seminole tongue. Tyler walked out and was coming up behind her, but he didn't see what she saw.

"Cheh moka is cheh," she said.

"Huh?" Tyler asked. She turned to him, wiped her eye.

"I said, I love you."

"Oh, well, I love you too, Sierra."

"No, I mean…I…."

He held her in a hug.

"Sierra and Tyler sitting in a tree, k-i-s-s-i-n—"

"Breanna, shut up!" she said in a clinched breath.

"Breanna?" Tyler asked.

"Oh uh… never mind."

Tyler stared into her eyes, placed his fingers on her chin, and held her face there. Brushing back her hair, he got closer.

BREEP BREEP!

The sudden annoying sound of her phone made both of them jump. She pulled her phone to her ear.

"Sierra?"

"Uncle Nelson, hi!"

"Honey, is everything okay? I just woke up from this weird dream about your family and some Indian guy in a creek."

She started laughing.

"Hello? Sierra?"

"I'm fine, Uncle Nelson."

"I'm coming up to get you."

"No, no Uncle Nelson, uh I'm okay here. I, uh, I think I wanna stay."

"Stay? Sierra, I don't know about that."

"But Uncle Nelson, I'm home. I was born here. I want to die here. Mr. Kettleman passed away. The town's going to have a funeral for him. I guess he must have thought the town took him for an old crazy, but OMG, Uncle Nelson, they loved him here."

"Yeah, I know. We'll talk about that, now that my big money deal with P-Mac is not going to happen. I hear she's in jail. I have to… oh… oh no.…"

"Have to run to the bathroom, Uncle Nelson?"

"I'll call you back."

CHAPTER NINETEEN

It was early morning. She didn't even know exactly what time it was. After all the craziness of the day before, Sierra had asked Tyler to take her back to the campsite. She stayed in one of the cabins and spent the night alone. She insisted on it. Sara and Benjamin had left the night before. They were arguing about the whole stay, and Sierra refunded their money. She was kind of glad to see them go. The sheriff told her that Wilbur had left the campsite to her in his will, with Nelson overseeing it until she turned twenty-one. And she gasped, "I'll be old by then!" Tyler respected her wish to stay alone, and after witnessing her take down "Frankenstein" with a simple hand gesture, he was sure that she could take care of herself. When he got home he told his grandmother the whole story.

"She's remarkable, Grams I think I'm in love with her."

✳ ✳ ✳

She washed her face and walked to the front door still wiping her face with a small hand towel, then stepped out on the porch. Her heel rested on a semi-loose board on the floor, and she looked down at it. She pressed her weight on it. It creaked.

"I'll have to get someone to fix that," she murmured to herself.

She stepped out and was shocked to find a small group of people standing out on the grounds, all of them Native American, and all of them staring at her.

"Sierra Russo." A tall Seminole stood closest to her doorway. His long, dark hair was tied in a braid behind his head. He had an acoustic guitar slung on his back.

"Yes?"

"We wish to thank you for keeping our home sacred. We, the council, doubted our brother Running Deer and his belief that you would honor our wishes. Thankfully you proved us all wrong. You are brave, you are a warrior—a true warrior of our tribe. Our home is now safe. We thank you, Sierra."

"Your home is my home." She smiled.

She stepped out off the porch to the soft, sandy ground, glancing around at all the people.

"You are entrusted with the task of watching over our home."

"And I will do so with pride."

"We trust that you will."

Not far away, a car was driving up to the half-burned and worn-down main cabin of Wilbur Kettleman. The small group of Seminoles turned, waved goodbye to her, and started walking into the lake. A small girl ran up to her, reached out, and held Sierra in a hug. "Thank you for saving my home." She smiled as she said it.

Then she ran back to her mother, and they all disappeared into the vast, clear water. Out past the view of them, she focused when she saw a blur on the banks across the lake. The wolf sat alone, calm, staring.

Unspoken conversation transpired between the two that no one else would have understood. She waved at it, then nodded. The huge, hairy animal also nodded, then walked back into the woods.

The car horn blew several sharp repetitive honks. She waved back, and Nelson stepped out of his car, ran up to his niece, and grabbed her in a hug. "Honey, are you okay?"

"Yes, Uncle Nelson. Actually, I don't think I have ever been better."

"Uh, who were you waving to?" He looked out at the water. No one was there, but she saw them wading into the cold waters of Old Indian Lake, all headed toward the depths in the middle.

"Nothing."

"Oh… okay. And do you want to explain to me why you spent the night here? I thought you were at Marjeanette's. I went there to find out that you'd spent the night here alone. Is that boy here somewhere?" He looked around, searching for the motorcycle.

"No, I'm alone, Uncle Nelson. I needed to be here—alone."

"Alone? Why?" he scratched his head.

"You know something, Uncle Nelson? I was thinking about your indigestion issue. You started having this about the time you started taking care of me, right?"

"Uh, well, you know I never thought of it that way, but yeah." He stepped away from her, looking back at the demolished cabin of Wilbur Kettleman.

"And it seems to me it usually flares up when we're talking about something that might upset you or me...."

"Uh, I guess...."

"I think I can fix your issue."

He put his arm around her. "Oh, now you're a doctor? You spend time in a clinic and now you're a medic?"

They laughed together and she looked out at the lake. Staring out into the calm glasslike water. The cloud above it had formed into an exact replica of Running Deer's face.

"Ilcep-ah-non-es-tchah." She smiled as she said it.

"Huh?"

"Nothing, Uncle Nelson. Let's go get some chocolate milk."

THE END

ilcep-ah-non-es-tchah = Good-Bye

© 2017 Rod Martinez